Dead Sometimes

A Jason Callahan Mystery

by Patricia Macomber

"There's one more interesting thing, Mr. Callahan," Dr. Walker offered up.

"As if that weren't enough."

"Chloe Marsh had a tonsillectomy at the age of seven. She also had an emergency appendectomy at the age of nineteen." Walker swallowed hard and narrowed his eyes a bit. "Both have been restored."

"What?" Jason groaned, sliding slowly out of his chair and allowing his eyes to widen.

"Her tonsils and her appendix. Both back."

"God."

"That's what I said." Sheriff Barnes placed his hands nervously on his hips and studied his shoes.

"I'd like to see her, if it's at all possible."

"She might still be awake. I'll take you to her."

Barnes and Jason followed Dr. Walker down the hall to an isolation room where Chloe was being kept. He paused for a moment before opening the door, steeling himself and causing Jason to wonder just how horrific the girl must appear.

He opened the door on a completely normal-looking young girl, however, and Jason exhaled loudly. "Knock, knock. Chloe? Are you awake?"

"Yes, Dr. Walker. I'm awake. Are you going to let me go home now?"

"Not just yet, Chloe. These men would like a word with you." He stepped aside, affording Jason a clear view of the girl.

ISBN 978-1-949914-91-7

For information address Crossroad Press at 141 Brayden Dr., Hertford, NC 27944
A Gordian Knot Books Production -Gordian Knot is an imprint of Crossroad Press.
www.crossroadpress.com

First edition

Chapter One

"Hey, hey, little bro!" Steve chirped as he swaggered through the door. His butt found the chair quickly and he sat smiling across the desk at Jason.

"Well, would you look at what the cat dragged in!" Jason laughed.

"How's the P.I. biz?" Steve asked, propping one ankle on the opposite knee and wiggling his foot.

Jason threw a suspicious sneer Steve's way. "It's all good. So, what do you want, Steve?"

"Want? Can't a guy drop in on his little brother just to say hi?" The smile that had won the hearts of juries and charmed a dozen beautiful women flashed past so quickly that Jason almost missed it.

"Sure. But he never does. So, I ask again...what do you want?"

"Could you run a check on this guy?" Steve flipped a card across the desk at him.

Jason picked up the card, glared at it through squinted eyes. His computer was already on, so he logged onto the website and typed in the guy's name and social. Within moments, the printer spat out six neat pages. Jason grabbed the papers and held them out to Steve. "There you go."

Steve smiled and grabbed the papers, scanning them quickly as his smile widened. "I knew it!"

"Care to tell me what this is all about?" Jason rocked in his chair and tried to avoid Steve's gaze.

"Sorry. Can't."

Jason nodded. "I understand."

"But thank you, little brother. I appreciate it." Steve stood, rolling the pages into a tube as he did so. He turned for the door, then snapped his fingers and turned back. "I almost forgot. I saw your lady friend this morning in that frou-frou coffee shop. You know, the…" he whistled the theme from 'Twilight Zone' "…psychic lady."

"Trina?" Jason perked up, though he tried to keep it out of his voice and expression. "I haven't seen her in ages. How's she doing?" His bid for nonchalance failed and he resorted to rocking in the chair again.

"She's still hot, if that's what you mean." Steve bore a crooked grin.

"It's not." The statement was flat but unconvincing.

"She said she was going to call you. I don't know about what." Steve watched Jason's face for hints of pleasure but found nothing. It's why they never played poker. "Well, thanks for the favor, little brother. See ya!"

Steve swept out the door and before Jason could stop himself, he glanced at the phone. Trina Dane. A blast from his recent past. He wondered briefly if he should just call her and get it over with. In the end, he decided that Steve was probably just yanking his chain and that a call to Trina would risk him being embroiled in another weird case…or worse.

The phone rang three times and still Barnes made no effort to answer it. On the fourth ring, his large hand slapped in its general direction, missing and striking the edge of the nightstand instead. On the fifth ring, his hand landed soundly on the receiver, long fingers wrapping around it, dragging it from its cradle and to his bed. It lay there, a useless tool, until someone's voice began repeating "Hello? Hello?" into the still air.

"What?" Barnes snorted in its general direction, only then making any effort to bring the phone to his ear. He rolled to his back as the phone made its arduous journey across the pillow.

"Sheriff? This is Ainsley. We've got us a murder-suicide down by Daniels Road. Or maybe a double homicide. We're not sure yet." Ainsley waited, silently, for his master's voice.

"So why the hell you calling me?" Barnes coughed, made the first abortive attempt at opening his eyes.

"Sir, it's because of one of the victims. Sheriff, it's Chloe Marsh."

Barnes was fully awake now, his eyes flapping open like broken roller shades and his elbow wedging him into a sitting position against the headboard. "What? Did you say it was Chloe?"

"I'm sorry, sir. But yeah."

"On my way. Daniels, you say?"

"Yes, sir."

He hung up then, making damn sure the receiver found its cradle and that the little red charging light came on. Then it was a mad scramble for his clothes and police gear. He didn't often carry weapons or cuffs anymore; didn't have much use for them since the promotion to Sheriff had turned him into a desk jockey. But he unlocked the gun cabinet and took out his Glock anyway, making sure to grab his cell phone, cuffs, and ID on his way out the door. If there was any press there, he wanted to look damn good and professional on the television.

The department car was parked in the driveway but he waited until he was clear of his neighborhood before he switched on the lights and sirens. No need to give his neighbors a midnight scare if he didn't have to. And he didn't.

Fifteen minutes of driving found him at the cluster of crime-scene vans and cruisers on Daniels Road. There were two cars, one man, two bodies. He picked that much up on his way to where Ainsley stood, hands on his hips, frowning as he watched the gentleman leaning on the car. And there was an ambulance.

"Bring me up to speed, Ainsley." He yawned voraciously.

"Well, we have Brenda Walsh right here. She dropped dead on the side of the road without a mark on her. They're still processing. Now, right here is Mr. Frank Porter…"

"Hello, Mr. Porter." Barnes offered a smile and a handshake, both of which were refused. Clearly, Mr. Porter had had better nights. He looked like he might throw up.

"Mr. Porter was on his way home from the airport when Chloe ran straight in front of his car. It was too sudden for him to slam on his brakes. She died on impact." Porter began to cry and Ainsley gave him a minute before he continued. "Chloe's at the hospital now. Mr. Porter called an ambulance right away."

Barnes screwed up his face and grabbed a handful of Ainsley's shirt. He dragged him a good distance away, then leaned in close to growl in the shorter man's ear. "If Chloe is dead, why the hell did she go to the hospital?" He waited for an answer, but Ainsley's mouth worked open and shut; that and nothing more. "Well, Ainsley? What the hell ain't you telling me?"

"It's hard to explain, sir. But the long and short of it is that Chloe's death is…somewhat in question."

Jason saw the outer door to his office open but couldn't see who was doing the opening. Joy was still at her desk. He could tell that from the delicate tapping of her nails on the keyboard. So, if she wasn't leaving, then someone must be coming in. It was a brilliant deductive leap.

"Go right on in, hon," Joy chirped and Jason felt his gut tighten. He could think of only one person with whom Joy might be friendly enough to call "hon."

"Knock, knock." And there stood Trina Dane, bane of his existence and owner of the most beautiful green eyes he had ever seen. She was decked out in flowing skirts and a standard issue peasant blouse, her arms dripping in bracelets and her fingers laden with rings. Her blonde hair was curlier than he remembered it. Her legs – or what he could see of them – were longer.

"Hi, Trina." Had his face lit up when he said that? He hoped not. "Long time no see."

She dropped into the chair, setting her huge carpet bag on the floor next to her and crossing those oh-so-long legs. "Not that long. It's been since…let me see…since that Jell-o attacked you at the casino."

"Yeah. Since that." He smiled for sure then and he couldn't be certain, but he thought he might have blushed. "So, what brings you to my humble office? Possessed pudding? Demons that look like poodles?"

"Nothing like that," she laughed, waving away his silliness with one jangling hand. "It's a homicide, straight up. Double. Maybe."

"Okay, Trina. It took you what? Five minutes? It took you five minutes to totally confuse me. Why don't you start at the beginning."

"It's like this. A story came over the wire. I know this because I pull all the notices out of the trash at work and go through them, just in case there's something weird."

"And there was something weird?"

"Yeah. See, there were these two women down in Florida…"

"Florida? Good God, Trina! What am I going to do about that?"

"Will you let me finish? And bear in mind, I am a psychic. I know when there's something wrong."

"So you keep telling me. Go on. Finish your story so I can get on with my life."

"Anyway, these two women are on their way home from the store, along a back road. They stop the car. There was a scuffle of some sort. One woman drops dead and the other runs out in front of a car and gets herself killed."

"That sucks for them. But the police are on it, right?"

"Yea, they are. But that's not the weird part."

"Okay, now we come to it. Out with it. What's the weird part?" He was half-amused, half-irritated. Right now, he couldn't decide which to be.

She sighed, drew in a long breath, held it for a moment, then released her words in a gust of wind. "The girl who was hit by the car was dead. Dead. And they took her to the hospital. Not the morgue or a funeral home. A hospital. Why would they do that?"

"I dunno." Jason leaned forward, lit a cigarette, watched her face turn sour. Victory.

"That's just it. They would never take a dead person to the hospital. Unless…"

"Wait for it…"

"Unless she wasn't dead. Or she was undead."

"Dear God!" His head hit the desk a little too hard.

"You know I'm right." Her eyes were squinted now, determined. She was leaning forward in the chair, hands tightly gripping the arms.

"Zombies? Really Trina?"

"Okay, you don't believe me? Here's another little tidbit. She never checked out. There's a record of her admission in the ER…but none of her being released."

"And you know this because…" Oh, surely there was something illegal going on here. Trina was a good person, but she just couldn't stop herself once that big old crazy train got rolling.

"Because I hacked the hospital computer system. Okay? You gonna call the cops and have me arrested now?"

"You know I'm not." He smiled then, in spite of himself.

"So, we have a dead girl in the hospital, not released. I held a little ceremony. There's something definitely wrong there. It's not in the news wires. It's not in the report. Oh, and there's been no obit. So, where's the girl?"

"With Elvis? How should I know? Look, Trina, I can't go running off across the country chasing every paranormal freakazoid news story you find."

"Two days in sunny Florida. Three tops. We'll have all the answers we need."

"No."

"But…"

"No. We don't have a client. I can't just go running off to Florida on my own dime. I'm running a business here, not a charity."

"Fine. I'll pay half."

"No. And if you were all that psychic, then you'd have known before you came here what my answer would be."

"But I did know." She smiled and winked at him and just like that, Jason was sunk.

"I said no," he tried.

"Jason!" She checked his face, frowned. That frown cut him to the core. Then she grabbed her bag and stood. "Well, I had to give it a try. I'll send you a postcard from Florida."

She was halfway to the door when Jason called to her. "Trina. Make sure when you talk to the cops that you don't bring up any of the weird stuff."

"Okay, Jason." She moved closer to Joy's desk.

Jason picked up his lighter, began turning it over in his fingers. "Trina."

"Yes, Jason?" She turned, her face showing hope.

"Make sure you ask them for a copy of the report."

"Sure."

"And get the autopsy, too. Both of them."

"Where do I get that at?" She blinked. Or was she batting her lashes at him? If only he knew.

"You can get that down at the coroner's office. Not the death certificate. The autopsy report, okay?"

"Sure, Jason, sure." She turned then, and made for the door, showing no signs of slowing.

Jason watched her grow smaller as she strode toward the door, fighting his inner demons like they were going to be beaten. "Aw, damn it!" he spat, tossing the lighter onto the desk and standing. "Trina! Wait up."

"We only found the body at eleven last night," Sheriff Barnes said as he chewed at the ear-piece of his sunglasses. He looked out of place in the white and gray, antiseptic surroundings of the morgue. "We haven't even gotten around to the autopsy yet."

"I'd like to be present for the autopsy, if that's okay with your M.E.," Trina requested.

Jason checked her face, scowling at her as if he'd just eaten something particularly awful. She waved him away with one hand, held low at her side and flicking in his general direction.

"I can't think of anything I'd like better than bending over a body with a lovely lady such as yourself." A rotund, balding man was ambling through the back door just then. He wore a white lab coat and munched voraciously on a sandwich.

"This is Dr. Tate, the county M.E. Bob, this is Private Investigator Jason Callahan and this is Trina Dane, his partner."

"Pleased to make your acquaintance." The man wiped his soggy hand on the leg of his trousers and offered it only to Trina. She smiled wanly and took it, wincing at the greasy feel of left-behind chicken and smears of mayonnaise.

"You said that you found no signs of foul play. Why then, were the police called in?" Jason eyed the pudgy man, wondering to himself how many of his corpses had been sewn back up with bits of ham and cheese clinging to their colons.

"Oh, we didn't call them in because of the victim, Mr. Callahan. We called them in because of the perpetrator." Dr. Tate swallowed hard and swiped at his greasy mouth once more. "Strangest damn thing..."

"Shut up, Bob."

"Well, the whole damn place is buzzing about it. They're gonna find out anyway."

"Dr. Tate here isn't known for his tact." Sheriff Barnes looked embarrassed, stricken.

"Well, that old axiom about fat people being jolly isn't always true." Jason shot a derisive look Tate's way. "Trina, why don't you and the good doctor get started on your autopsy. Sheriff Barnes, I'd like to see the crime scene, if that's at all possible."

"Sure thing. We had the car towed but the whole scene's been cordoned off. Hasn't rained yet, so everything should still be pretty fresh."

Jason leaned close to Trina for a moment, his mouth crooking into a grin. "Keep your eye on that one, Trina. If he shoves something in your hand, more than likely it won't be a scalpel."

Jason turned with a flourish and strode cockily to the door, Trina sneering at him playfully as he went.

Sheriff Barnes led Jason to his patrol car. The lot behind the combination Sheriff's Department, Morgue and jail was paved in dirt and so it was apt to shift a bit to the east or west, depending on which way the wind was blowing on any given day. Luckily, Florida's renowned afternoon showers had been strangely absent the past few days, so the dirt wasn't nearly as compacted or as dimpled with puddles.

Barnes wove the car through the maze of other cruisers, then made his way onto the downtown Ft. Myers streets. This part of town hadn't changed much in the past thirty years or so and Barnes could make his way through the area blindfolded. A few of the streets had been made one-way in the last two years, adding to the confusion and detracting from the amount of shoppers who ventured out of the mainstream malls and down to the quaint shops, but it was still very much the smallish town he had been born into.

"Who was it that found the body?" Jason asked, startling Barnes from his nostalgic reverie.

"That would be Frank Porter. He owns a house down that way and nearly ran over the body on his way home from the airport."

"Do you see many murders out in this area?" Jason hadn't meant that as an insult; he was merely curious.

"We're not exactly the shit-splat town everyone thinks we are. I mean, we're not nearly so big as New York, but we hold our own."

"I wasn't implying..."

"We see plenty of murders. Lots of drug traffic and...yes... even a few hard boiled cases, like the DEA bombing couple of years back. I've been with the Sheriff's Department for over thirty years, and I ain't never seen nothing like this."

Barnes wheeled the car onto a six-lane road, passing a sizable shopping mall/movie theater complex. Everything here was low and sprawling, laced with palm trees. And it was oh, so flat!

"This is Daniel's Road. Right up ahead is where the perp was hit. Soon as we get down this dirt road, you'll see where we found the other body."

Barnes eased the cruiser onto the right shoulder of the road and then cut the engine. He threw open the door and stepped out onto the hard dirt, finger-pressing the crease in his pants. Hands on his hips, he squinted against the blinding sunlight.

"Right there is where the car stopped. We're still not sure why. And then they both got out of the car."

Jason turned toward the man, his demeanor suddenly becoming more menacing, more impatient. "Why don't you just talk me through the whole event, as far as you know it, that is."

Barnes ripped the Ray Bans from his face and glared angrily at Jason. "Now, lookit here, Mr. Callahan. I may not be a hot shot big city detective, but I know how to conduct an investigation. I'm what folks around here call a 'cracker', which means I'm Florida born and bred. Third generation, as a matter of fact. And I'm second generation Sheriff's Department. My own daddy served under the great Snag Thompson when he was Sheriff. So, you may not think I've got the brains to pour piss out of a boot with the instructions on the heel, but I *know* how to conduct my investigations. I'll walk you through this whole damn thing step by step and then you tell me what's what."

Jason paled in the face of this man, who had a good four inches and a muscular hundred pounds on him. He wasn't about to start discussing the finer points of DNA tests or ground compaction tests with the man. "I'm sorry. No offense intended."

"Offense taken." He replaced his Ray Bans and stalked off in the direction of the first crime area. "According to witnesses at the local Evermart, Chloe Marsh locked her keys in her car. Brenda Walsh, who happens to be a cashier at that self-same Evermart was leaving work and offered Chloe a ride home to get her spare keys. Witnesses have them leaving together in Brenda's car at roughly six-thirty that night."

"How did Chloe expect to get into her apartment to get her spare keys if her other keys were locked in the car?"

Barnes turned on him with eyes that told Jason he was the dumbest toad ever set on the Earth. "Because, Mr. Callahan, her landlady...who just happens to live on the premises...has a set of keys."

"Just asking." Jason threw up his hands defensively and squelched a smile.

"Anyway, they left the Evermart and headed for Chloe's apartment building. It's just a mile or so west of here on Daniels. They would have come down Six Mile Cypress...the back way. Why the hell they stopped here has got me stumped. There wasn't any problem with Brenda's car. It turned right over when the tow truck came to haul it off.

"We can place Chloe in the car, not only because of eye witness accounts, but also because of the cigarette butts. The ashtray was full of Doral Lights, which Brenda smokes. There was one Winston butt at the front of the ashtray. It had the same lipstick on it that Chloe always wears.

"When they got here, both of the girls evidently got out of the car. You can see Brenda's footprints...they're the ones with the flat soles and the heart imprints. She always wears those same nurse's shoes. Chloe's are the L.A. Gear Walkers. Both sets of prints lead over to here..." He walked several feet south and crossed the road. "...where there appears to have been a scuffle of some sort."

Jason stooped down and examined the scrambled foot prints. There was clearly quite a scuffle, then both sets of prints led off toward Daniel's Road. Jason followed the myriad of prints toward the paved road.

"They took off running sometime after the scuffle. We can tell that because of the soil compaction and distortion of the prints." With that, he shot a sneer at Jason. "And right here, Brenda collapsed. She fell face down on the dirt for no apparent reason and that's just where Frank Porter found the body."

Jason crouched down again and studied the outlines of a woman's body. It was sprawled out considerably, as though she had made no attempt at breaking her fall. There was a long, deep scorch mark in the dirt, beginning at about where the woman's mouth would have been and ending approximately five feet from there.

"What's this?" Jason inquired, turning his sun-beaten eyes up to Barnes.

"Ah, you noticed that, did you? Well, that one's quite a puzzler to me, too. I had some soil samples taken to the lab, but all they could tell me was that the sand had been melted. Said it could only be melted like that at temperatures of over a thousand degrees."

Jason poked at the deposit with one tentative finger and overturned a shard of glass. He produced a plastic bag from his pocket and held it up for Barnes' inspection. "Mind?"

"Be my guest."

Jason placed the shard of glass in the bag, sealed it, and pushed it back into his pocket. "So, Brenda fell right here, but Chloe's footprints lead off toward the road."

"Yup. She ran on, I guess not knowing that Brenda wasn't after her no more. According to the guy driving the car...Frank Porter...and two eye witnesses driving the opposite direction, she just ran right in front of his car. Didn't even notice that it was there. Porter was just coming from the airport. He's a computer salesman in town for a convention. He was headed for the Holiday Inn in his rented car when the whole thing happened. You ain't never seen anybody so crushed in all your life."

"So, Porter didn't know either of the women. Did the two women know each other?"

"Only so much as a routine customer and a cashier can know each other. Anyway, the car struck her doing fifty, which is the legal limit ri'cheer."

"And she died on impact?"

"Well...sort of. Porter got out of the car right off and checked for a pulse. He said she didn't have one then and the paramedics didn't find one when they came onto the scene. But Porter swears that just before they loaded her onto the gurney, Chloe's eyes shot open and she looked right at him. Gave him a mighty big case of the heeby jeebies, that did."

"But they pronounced her dead once they got her to the hospital? She never regained consciousness?" Jason felt something mysterious tickling at the base of his brain. Barnes knew something that he wasn't letting on and Jason had to know what it was.

Barnes looked uncomfortable, his face red, whether from heat or embarrassment, Jason couldn't be sure. The man swiped at the back of his neck and studied the ground. "Well, now, I'll just let the doctor tell you about that part. I can give you all the where-fors and hows-comes, but I'm no physician. She was taken to Gulf Coast. It's right over there."

"Then let's go. We're burning daylight here."

The two men walked back to the cruiser. Jason knew for sure he wouldn't get any more out of Barnes just then. The whole incident had clearly upset the sheriff enormously, so he didn't push.

They pulled into the parking lot of Gulf Coast Hospital and climbed from the car. Barnes stood for a moment, wiping the sweat off his brow with a clean, white handkerchief.

"Woo! It's hotter than a fish turd on a sand bar out here. Come on. Let's get in out of the heat."

Jason smirked at the man's metaphor, lowering and shaking his head. He followed Barnes inside the cool building and waited while he spoke to the nurse at the front desk.

"We're in luck. Dr. Walker just happens to be in right now."

Barnes took off down the hall without further edification. Jason followed dutifully behind him, anxious to get at the really exciting portion of this mystery, such as whether or not Chloe Marsh really was dead. It was why Trina had made him come. It was the reason he wasn't, at that exact moment, sitting at Yankee Stadium enjoying a beer.

They went up to the second floor, then stopped at the nurse's station. Barnes smiled at the young woman and leaned flirtatiously across the counter. "Good morning, darlin'. Would you happen to know where Dr. Walker is at the moment?"

The young woman batted her long lashes at him and smiled coyly. Obviously, the two were acquainted. "He's with a patient at the moment. But he should be done in a sec, if you'd like to wait."

"It would be my pleasure," Barnes offered, lingering for a moment to study the girlish nurse's comely form. His voice had gone soft and gentle and the whole thought of Barnes in a romantic tryst made Jason shudder visibly.

Jason strode over to a bank of chairs and dropped into one, feeling suddenly tired and exhilarated both at once. He was itching to get at Barnes' secret; could see himself shaking the man until he gave it up.

Within moments, a tall, serious-looking gent appeared from around the corner. He was writing something on a clipboard and very nearly collided with Barnes as he approached the desk.

"Dr. Walker, Sheriff Barnes would like a word with you."

Walker looked up from his copious notes and grinned a bit.

"Ah, Barnes! Good to see you again. What can I do you for?"

"I'm here with Jason Callahan. He's a New York P.I. who's here investigating the incident for the victim's family." He motioned in Jason's direction and Jason stood up to greet the man. "He'd like to hear what you know about the Marsh girl."

Walker's face grew suddenly pale and taut. "Why don't we go into the lounge where we can talk in private." He snapped his fingers twice and the nurse produce another chart, complete with x-rays and other pertinent attachments. Walker tucked it under his arm, and walked away.

Everyone had grown so deadly silent and morose at the mention of Chloe's name that Jason could already feel the goose-flesh crawling up his back. He followed the two men, joining in on their silence and sense of foreboding.

"I was the attending physician last night when Chloe came in," Walker began, shutting the door and straightening his back. "These are her x-rays."

He held them up for Jason's perusal, indicating points of interest with one long index finger.

"You can see here that she had a very severe skull fracture. And here, her spinal column was completely severed at the base of her skull. If that first injury hadn't killed her, one of the other two would. Here, it clearly shows a fragment of her rib stabbing right through her heart."

Walker reclaimed the x-rays quickly and shoved them unceremoniously back onto their manila envelope. "Now that you've seen them, forget you ever saw them. Because as far as I'm concerned, they don't even exist."

"What makes you say that, Dr. Walker?" Jason had that creepy feeling again, the one that made his privates crawl and his hair stand on end.

Walker leaned against the wall and stared off into time and space. "Chloe Marsh was hit by a car at approximately seven o'clock last evening. The gentleman who hit her swears he couldn't raise a pulse at the scene. Ten minutes later, when the paramedics arrived, they also couldn't raise a pulse. Bear in mind that, for all intents and purposes, that woman was already dead for ten minutes.

"She was then brought to the emergency room. That was at seven-twenty-three. By this time, she's been dead at least twenty-three minutes. I saw her two minutes later. I pronounced her dead at that time. We sent for an orderly to take her to the morgue. She's dead now some thirty minutes."

"No attempt was made to revive her?" Jason asked stupidly.

"She was dead on impact Mr. ..."

"Callahan."

"Mr. Callahan. There's no sense in reviving a person who's been dead that long. As I was saying, by the time the orderly arrived, forty minutes had passed. He stopped outside at the nurse's desk to sign the papers. By this time, poor Chloe has been dead for forty-five minutes. Dead." His face was a mask of severity and humbling sorrow as he said this last.

"I happened to be standing at the nurse's desk when he arrived with her. I was signing a medication order. Chloe, by this time, has been dead for nearly an hour. We were standing there...all of us...the nurse, the orderly, me. All of a sudden, out of the blue, Chloe springs up into a sitting position and sucks in this great big breath. Her eyes are open and she's staring right straight ahead like she's seeing something the rest of us aren't. And then, after several seconds of consciousness, she just collapses onto the gurney again. She's still alive, but comatose."

Jason suddenly felt like he wanted to run, out of the hospital for sure, all the way back to New York perhaps. "What you're telling me is that, after being dead for damn near an hour, this woman suddenly came back to life? And there were no attempts made to revive her? It was spontaneous?"

Walker kneaded his hands fiercely and stared straight into Jason's disbelieving eyes. "That is precisely what I'm saying, Mr. Callahan. As time passed, she started regaining consciousness more frequently and for longer periods of time. We ran some more tests on her, to see how the hell she could still be alive. She sustained not one, not two, but three certainly fatal injuries. And she's here to tell about it."

"What did the follow-up tests show?"

"They showed that her spine had healed itself. They also showed that her heart and rib were back in their normal positions. The only thing that was not completely healed was her skull fracture. If you look closely, you can still make out a faint line where the fracture hasn't yet completely healed."

Jason sank back into a nearby chair and ran one trembling hand through his sandy hair. His mind was reeling with the enormity of this whole thing.

"There's one more interesting thing, Mr. Callahan," Dr. Walker offered up.

"As if that weren't enough."

"Chloe Marsh had a tonsillectomy at the age of seven. She also had an emergency appendectomy at the age of nineteen." Walker swallowed hard and narrowed his eyes a bit. "Both have been restored."

"What?" Jason groaned, sliding slowly out of his chair and allowing his eyes to widen.

"Her tonsils and her appendix. Both back."

"God."

"That's what I said." Sheriff Barnes placed his hands nervously on his hips and studied his shoes.

"I'd like to see her, if it's at all possible."

"She might still be awake. I'll take you to her."

Barnes and Jason followed Dr. Walker down the hall to an isolation room where Chloe was being kept. He paused for a moment before opening the door, steeling himself and causing Jason to wonder just how horrific the girl must appear.

He opened the door on a completely normal-looking young girl, however, and Jason exhaled loudly. "Knock, knock. Chloe? Are you awake?"

"Yes, Dr. Walker. I'm awake. Are you going to let me go home now?"

"Not just yet, Chloe. These men would like a word with you." He stepped aside, affording Jason a clear view of the girl.

She was a small, slight girl; hardly a hundred pounds dripping wet. She had intense, compelling brown eyes and the longest, silkiest blond hair that Jason had ever seen. Her skin was as pale as the moon and nearly as luminescent. Just looking at her, Jason would never have guessed that she'd spent a sick day in her life.

She straightened in the bed, trying to offer as strong a presence as she could. "Hello, Dawg," she giggled demurely.

Barnes met Jason's bemused glance, blushing in the face of it. "She's the only one allowed to call me that."

"My folks used to live next door to the Barnes' when I was little. I couldn't say 'Barnes', so I just named him after the Deputy Dawg in my cartoons."

"And it stuck, too, darlin'. I was at the Academy for six months before I got those bozos to stop calling me that."

They shared a mutual laugh, then Barnes bent to kiss her forehead. "How you feelin', little love?"

"Much better. I can't understand why they're still keeping me here."

"They just want to make sure you're feelin' all better before they sic you on the world again." He drew up a chair and eased into it. It groaned in protest of the sudden burden. "If you're feelin' up to it, we'd like to ask you a few questions."

"Must be dang serious. You brought reinforcements." She shot a questioning glance at Jason.

"This is Mr. Callahan. He's a private investigator from New York."

"Hello," he said, offering one wary hand to her.

"Nice to meet you, Mr. Callahan. My, aren't I hot stuff, rating my very own personal P.I.!"

Jason pulled up a chair, content to let Sheriff Barnes take the lead.

"Chloe, darlin', what in creation were you doing with Brenda Walsh last night?"

Chloe suddenly grew pale, if it was possible to achieve a paler shade of white. "I locked my stupid keys in the car again. Brenda came out just as I was fixin' to call for a cab. She offered me a lift back to my apartment. Said she would bring me back to my car once I got my spare keys."

"And why did you stop on Palomino?"

"Lord knows. We were driving along, listening to the radio and making small talk. All of a sudden, she just pulls onto the dirt road without saying a word. She stopped the car and turned to look at me and then, without so much as a fare-thee-well, she grabs me by the throat. She's digging her fingers into my neck and all and I wondered to myself just why the heck she was doing that.

"Well, I thought she was going to kill me. I couldn't breathe a lick and my hands were starting to fold up and I couldn't make them open again. So, I just put my foot right on her chest and shoved for all I was worth. She went a flying back against the other door and I just jumped out of that car.

"I ran down the road a few feet but she was on me like white on rice. We fought for a bit, but I finally managed to get free of her again. I swear to God, Dawg, she had the weirdest look in her eye. She never said a single thing, but I swear she looked like that Charles Manson guy you always see the stories about.

"So, I got free of her again and I ran down the road, looking to flag down a car. I guess that's when I got hit, 'cause I don't remember a thing after that."

Barnes leaned back in his chair and placed his beefy hands on his knees. "And you got no idea how Brenda might have ended up dead?"

Chloe's eyes flew open and her jaw went slack. "Dead? Brenda's dead?"

"Sorry, darlin'. I thought you already knew."

"I had no idea." She looked as though she might cry at any moment. Jason took it to be sincere. She looked at the way Barnes was eyeing her, then began to shake her head slowly. "Now, you just wait one darn minute, Dawg. You don't think I killed that girl, now do you?"

"Calm down, Chloe. All we're saying right now is that Brenda died on that road last night and you were the only other person there."

"I swear, Dawg. I didn't kill her. There's no way I killed that girl. I put my foot in her chest and pushed her off me. I even struggled with her for a bit. But there's no way in heck I could ever kill anybody."

"It's okay, Chloe. We believe you. We just have to find out everything you know so we can figure out how she did die. Catch my drift?"

She was beginning to calm down a bit now, though her eyes still looked frantic. "I know. You're just doing your job. But I've told you everything I know. Believe you me, if I knew anything that would help you, I'd say so."

"Okay, honey pot," he chuckled, patting her leg with one large hand. "I've heard all I need for now. Would you mind talking to Mr. Callahan here for a while? I'm sure he has some questions of his own."

She looked cautiously over at Jason, sizing him up. "I guess so. But I don't know what else I can tell you that I haven't already."

"I'll just leave you two alone. Take it easy on her, Callahan. She's had a rough go of it."

"Not to worry, Sheriff."

Jason and Chloe watched as Barnes shuffled out of the room, closing the door behind him. Jason returned his gaze to Chloe, who was now staring at him with all the ferocity and calculated cunning of a cornered beast.

Chapter Two

"Do you know what happened to you last night?" Jason asked Chloe.

Her mood had lightened somewhat. She was at least less intense. "Of course I know what happened. I died last night. It's not like it never happened before."

Jason was taken aback at that remark. He sat back in his chair and cast a wary eye on her. "It's happened before?"

"Yeah. Twice."

Suddenly, he leaned forward, listening intently and staring at her. "Tell me what you saw on those other two occasions."

"Let's see, the first time was a drug overdose. I was only nineteen at the time. I was kinda wild, you know what I mean? My dad died right after I was born, so it was always just me and Mama. She died two days after my nineteenth birthday and I kinda went off the deep end. I was at a party with my boyfriend. We were smoking some pot and drinking some beers. Then, this guy shows up with some pills. He tells me they're real mild, that they won't hurt me. So, I took some of those, too. I can remember sitting there, just listening to 'em all talk. And all of a sudden, I started getting this tunnel vision and they started sounding all far away and stuff. The very next thing I know, I'm all laid out on the floor with everybody staring down at me and stuff."

"Tell me about while you were dead. What did you see?"

She looked at him, wondering if he already knew what she would say. Most people looked at her like she was crazy when she told the story and she thought he just might fall into that same frame of mind.

"Well, I know this sounds just like the stories you always hear on the talk shows and all, but I really did go into a tunnel. There was a really bright light at the end of the tunnel and I just kept drifting up toward that light. But before I could get there, I guess I was sent back or something, 'cause I just started floating right back down to my body."

"Did you see your body while you were out of it?"

"No. Huh-uh. I guess I missed that part. Anyways, I woke up there on the floor and everybody was telling me that I had died. My girlfriend...who just happens to have been a nurse... told me that I swallowed my tongue and that my heart stopped and I quit breathing. She said I was dead for something like five minutes. They were all wondering whether or not to call the EMS, on account of the drugs and stuff. Luckily for them, I came back before they actually had to call."

"You didn't see or talk to anybody while you were gone?"

"Nope. Not a soul. But I really changed after that. I quit doing the drugs and drinking and smoking. Well, the smoking never really took, but I quit the rest of it. I figured...hey...I've come back once, maybe I ought not to press my luck. I guess you could say I got kinda pious. The second time cured me of that, though. After that second time, I figured that God, or whoever had control over such things, just wouldn't let me die. I figured that I was practically indestructible, if you catch my drift."

"Tell me about that second time. Was it the same?"

"Just the same. I was out in the garage, fixing to sand some cabinets so I could stain them. But my stupid boyfriend didn't bother to tell me that the sander had a short in it. I latched onto that dang thing and it bit right into me. I was thinking it was just like those cartoons you always see. You know, your hand just won't let go of the thing, even though you know it's hurting you. My hand was locked tight onto that sucker and I just watched the ceiling pass by as I fell onto the floor. Same as before, I went into that tunnel. And before you ask...no...I didn't see my body that time, either. I saw the light and the tunnel and I went up through the tunnel. But the light sent me back before I ever got into it. I woke up about two hours later with a big old headache and a tingling in my arm that lasted darn near a month."

"How about this time? Was it the same as the others?"

She screwed up her face and thought hard about this for a moment before answering. "Well, it kinda was and it kinda wasn't. See, I don't remember being hit by the car, but I remember starting up through the tunnel. Not long after I went into the tunnel, I was sent...quick as a lick...back to my body. I opened my eyes and was staring at this man stooped over me and feeling my neck. Then, I just went right back into that tunnel again." She broke off into a shudder, her eyes pressing tightly closed against whatever she was recalling.

"Are you all right? Do you want me to call the doctor?"

She swallowed hard and struggled to speak. "No. I just get these headaches every now and again. They don't last long, but they're real doozies just the same."

"We can always pick this up later." He felt horribly sorry for her. The poor girl had had such a hard life, and now this.

"I'd rather just get it over with, if it's all the same to you."

"All right. Go on."

"Well, as soon as I went back into that tunnel, I started seeing things. Not with my eyes, of course, since I didn't have eyes to look through right then. But I got impressions of things, dark things, clinging to the sides of the tunnel and waiting to just grab me. I got almost to the end of the tunnel, where there was still light, but when it was time to pass through, something stopped me. Mind you, it wasn't like before, when I got sent back. Something...some force...wasn't letting me in there. So, I just hung out. I was floating there until I was sucked back down into my body. And ever since I got back, things just haven't felt right."

"What do you mean, they haven't felt right?"

"I can't really explain it any better than that. It's just that my body, it doesn't feel the same to me anymore. It's like I'm in somebody else's body. It's like I don't have complete control over it anymore. As my mama might say, I'm not her toe-headed, blue-eyed angel anymore."

Jason snickered in spite of his best efforts to prevent it. "But Chloe, your eyes are brown."

"Oh, no, Mr. Callahan," she giggled demurely. "My eyes are and always have been blue."

Jason gaped at her in bemused disbelief, then reached into the drawer of the table next to the bed. He held forth a small hand mirror, allowing her to inspect her reflection in it. "Take a look, Chloe. Your eyes are as brown as Bambi's."

She gazed into the mirror, the smile sliding off her face as sudden dawning crossed it. "Oh my God! My eyes are brown." She checked his response; was not bolstered by it.

"Do you wear contacts?"

"No. I can't wear them. They hurt. I have to wear glasses all the time 'cause my eyesight's so..." The mirror slid from her thin fingers as she stared out the window at the trees outside.

"What is it Chloe? What's the matter?"

"My eyes. I can see perfectly."

Jason blinked at her, unsure of what to make of this. "Maybe it was something that happened during the accident. Perhaps the blow you sustained to your head..."

"Bull! You and I both know that's not true. Any more than donkeys can fly. Something's happened to me. I can feel it. But it has nothing to do with the accident."

They passed a few moments in nervous silence, then Chloe risked speaking again. "Why so many questions? I mean, Dawg's interested in me 'cause of what happened to Brenda. But why all the metaphysical stuff? What's your angle in this?"

He chanced a boyish grin at her, then leaned in as if he were about to share a coveted secret with her. "I'll tell you something. I'm not your run-of-the-mill private detective."

"You're not?" Her surprise was genuine. So was her smile.

"Nope. I'm in charge of all the...shall we say...strange cases. Anything that doesn't seem to have a logical explanation, my partner and I step in and we try to find an illogical explanation."

She tittered at him, suddenly liking this charming, boyish man. "And I'm a strange case, huh?"

"Well, you were dead for almost an hour. I can't say we see that every day."

She crossed her arms over her chest and cocked her head at him. "So, do you think I killed Brenda?"

"Actually, I don't. I think Brenda had some sort of heart attack or a stroke or something. If you're telling the truth, then you couldn't possibly have killed her."

"I am telling the truth, Mr. Callahan. I swear."

"I believe you, Chloe."

"And what do you think is happening to me? Based on your experience with such things, that is."

"I can't really say just yet. But I'll make you a deal. As soon as I've figured it out, you'll be the first one I tell."

Jason gave her a sideward wink and then sidled out of the room. Sheriff Barnes was waiting for him in the hall, leaning over the high desk and talking rather animatedly with the nurse while he browsed her form. Jason sneaked up behind him and waited a few moments, unnoticed by either of them. Then, he cleared his throat loudly and waited for the blushing to begin.

"Done with Chloe already, eh? My how you big city boys do rush."

"There really wasn't a lot to say. I'd like to ask you a few questions, though."

Barnes leaned casually against the wall and stuck his hands in his pockets. "Shoot."

"I'd like to know more about Chloe. Her background."

"Sure. She's Florida born and bred like me, though she mostly grew up in a little town just east of here called Lehigh Acres. She was a quiet kid, good student, never gave anybody any problems."

"Does she have any particular religious affiliation?"

"Naw. Her ma was devout Catholic and her dad was a Methodist. Neither of 'em ever had much time to see to things religious. She had a mild go 'round with booze and drugs and such after her ma died. Hell, I even picked her up on a DUI once. Didn't make a case of it. Just drove the kid home and tucked her in. All that was just because she fell in with a bad crowd is all. That damn kid she was dating wasn't worth two nubbins of goat manure, I can tell you that. Doing time in the Federal pen for kidnapping and rape."

"What's she been like since then?"

"Oh, hell! That girl's been squeaky clean. Works two jobs,

hasn't touched the drugs or booze in years. She donates blood regularly. Donates time for the Meals on Wheels, the habitat for Humanity. Anybody needs help, she's the first one on the scene. Still can't figure hows come she never got hitched up with some nice fella. Got a lot to offer, that girl does."

"As much as that pretty nurse?" He jerked his head comically to indicate the little blond.

"Ah, hell, boy! I'm married. I ain't dead."

Jason chuckled deep in his throat and straightened to leave. "Thanks, Sheriff Barnes. You've been a big help."

Jason walked through the door of the morgue, laden with papers and the like. He was whistling, which told Trina that something had really piqued his interest. He strode right up to her and thrust out his chin, smiling against her disgusted frown.

"So, how did we make out on that autopsy?"

"You're in an awfully good mood, Jason. What happened? Did you uncover an alien conspiracy to overthrow the government?"

"Better."

"You finally beat Virtual Fighter!"

"Very funny, Trina. Actually, I've happened upon a young girl who just happens to be very talented. At dying and coming back to life."

"That's interesting. I've happened upon one who isn't."

"What did you find out?"

"For starters, Brenda Walsh died because all her neural synapses had become fused together. By the time she got into that car with Chloe Marsh, she had barely enough brain left to blink."

Jason whistled through his teeth and leaned on Dr. Tate's desk. "Anything else?"

"It's never enough for you, is it, Jason?" She wet her lips and pressed on. "Her heart was severely enlarged, there was enough adrenaline in her system to power a battleship and, from all the physical evidence Dr. Tate can gather, her temperature was high enough to fry an egg on her forehead."

"No signs of drugs? Disease?"

"No drugs, no alcohol, no disease of any kind. Other than her apparent heart condition and brain dysfunction, that girl was as healthy as a horse."

"Curiouser and curiouser. So, why did you want to watch the autopsy anyway?"

"I wanted to see if anything came out of the body."

"And did it?"

"No." She chewed her lips for a second and stared off into space. "So, was Chloe able to offer you any explanations?"

"I'm afraid not. She got into the car with Brenda. The next thing she knew, Brenda had stopped the car and was trying to choke her to death. She managed to fight her off and make a break for it, but Brenda caught her again. As Chloe was running toward the main road to get help, Brenda apparently just collapsed, dead."

"Great. So there's an eyewitness but she didn't see anything."

"Chloe's quite an interesting girl. Do you know she's died three times and come back to life each time? And all without any form of medical assistance."

She studied his face for a minute, gauging his sincerity in this. "You're not kidding, are you?"

"Not a bit. This time, she was dead for nearly an hour. Three people will testify to that in a court of law. All of a sudden, she just sits right up in bed and starts breathing again. What do you make of that, Trina?"

"I think the three people who declared her dead were wrong."

"Not a chance. One of those people was a bona fide medical doctor. And, he had x-rays taken to help with the autopsy. She had a severe skull fracture and her spinal cord was severed just below the head. But the real kicker is that one of her ribs was broken and the fragment penetrated her heart."

"Any one of those things would be enough to kill her. But all three?" Now, Jason had her undivided attention.

"Know what else? This sweet girl, whose eyes used to be blue and terribly near-sighted, now has brown eyes and twenty-twenty vision."

Trina raised her eyebrows and pulled down the corners of her mouth. "What does she think caused it?"

"I'm not sure she even has a clue. If she does, then she's not telling."

Trina tossed back her long blonde hair and screwed up her face in thought. "I can think of a lot of things that would be responsible for Chloe's rejuvenation, and a few that could explain her change in eye color."

"For example?" He was sure he didn't want to hear any of her theories. Mostly, Trina's theories led to facts and those led to him being severely injured in some way.

"Well, a possession would explain the change in eye color and would definitely explain why Brenda would suddenly attack her, and then simply drop dead."

"How's that?"

"Well, the possessor left Brenda's body in a sad state, then transferred into Chloe."

"Happens a lot, does it?" His tone was mocking now, his smile lacking mirth.

"More than you'd think."

"Well, that's very interesting, Trina. But the fact is that we don't really have a case here. There's no sign of foul play involved in Brenda's death. And, although Chloe certainly is fascinating, we can't possibly justify staying here and trying to solve the mystery of her rebirth."

Trina shuffled her feet and adopted that "ah-gee" attitude. "I know." Suddenly, she looked up at him, her face stuck somewhere between impish and coy. "Would it help if I had a piece of really weird physical evidence?"

He studied her face again, trying to decide which answer would get him in the least trouble. "Do you?"

"I do." Her hand darted into his coat pocket and produced the plastic bag containing the charred sand. "This! Ha!" She dangled the bag in front of his face then, sneering and shaking it back and forth.

Jason's smile faded, his shoulders slumped. "I truly hate that you're psychic."

"I know." She sounded so pleased with herself, so imperious.

"Now, tell me about this little beauty."

"It was found at the crime scene. It began where Brenda's mouth would have been and extended five feet in the direction that Chloe was running."

Trina eyed it distastefully. "Looks like glass."

"Sand, Trina. It used to be sand." He watched as her confused eyes lifted to meet his. "All that aside, I think we should go back to New York and let the lab boys analyze it. Until something strange turns up, there's nothing keeping us here."

"You're right, Jason, of course. But it's kinda late now. I suggest that we get a good night's sleep and head for home in the morning."

"Sounds like a plan."

"Buy me dinner?" she asked girlishly.

"To quote Sheriff Barnes, "Do bears shit in the woods?'" Jason leaned against the desk again, a self-satisfied grin gracing his face.

The air was thick and hot and the air never stirred. Yankee that he was, Jason was reluctant to leave the comfort of the air conditioned hotel building just to get dinner. Most people would love a tropical vacation, but not Jason. He loved the cold, the snow, the gray of the sky. Sun felt unnatural to him. It burned his skin.

Jason and Trina enjoyed a peaceful dinner in the hotel restaurant, followed by an early bedtime. The county M.E. listed Brenda's cause of death as natural causes and Jason's mind was at ease concerning the whole affair. Although there was certainly something strange about a girl who could suffer such severe injuries and still manage to reanimate herself, it was neither strange enough nor dangerous enough to warrant his staying on the case.

At breakfast the next morning, Jason was quiet, nearly sullen. He knew that Trina wanted to stay and poke the case with a stick. She was the one who had first smelled something supernatural in the so-called common car accident. She would not be happy to leave.

Jason ordered, stewed over his coffee as he sought a way to broach the subject with her that wouldn't incite a screaming match. Halfway through his eggs and bacon, he wiped at his mouth, cleared his throat, and settled the napkin gently in his lap. "I think we should leave right after breakfast."

Trina's eyes shot up, scoured his face and wrinkled at the corners. "Leave? For where?"

"Home."

"Home? Are you kidding me? You still want to leave?" She choked down a bite of hash browns and frowned. "But we haven't solved the case. We still have no idea..."

"The police will solve the case, Trina." He stared her down, trying not to blink.

"But the girl...Chloe...And that wicked scorch mark." She swallowed again, squeezed her eyes tightly closed for a second before continuing. "Jason, there's something very weird going on here. Aside from the fact that we found a girl who can't die, we found a possible case of possession."

"That's your theory. Not mine. And whatever happened, the police will handle it."

"The police *can't* handle it!" she shouted, throwing her napkin on the table and sneering at him. "Do you think they'll even admit if they find a malevolent spirit? Or that they can get rid of it?"

"No, but..."

"No. They can't. I can."

"Trina, I don't want to have an argument with you in this... very public place." He looked around him, aware for the first time that they were center-stage, in the middle of a well-attended dramedy. "I came down here of my own free will. I'm not getting paid and we don't have an actual client. What I do have is an office and real clients with real money that I need to pay my bills. And unless I miss my guess, you do too."

She sighed dramatically and sank back into her chair, pouting. "I know," she said softly.

"I'm sorry. I have to go home and do some paid work. I can't afford to be the White Knight, holed up in some Best Western castle until something weird happens. If it does."

"Fine." She pushed her plate away, prepared to maintain her sullen mood for the rest of the day. "But mark my words, that girl is possessed by someone or something and eventually, that someone or something will have to be driven out. And I'm the only one who can do it."

"I know." He tried to smile, to placate her into forgiving him. "Let's just pay the tab and get going."

Once Jason had dropped Trina at her house, he drove the sand sample to the lab, then went immediately to check his messages. He had several minor details to clear up, then he would have the rest of the day free to spend in a vegetative state in front of the TV. If his luck held out, there might be a good ball game on.

The next morning, as Jason was eating breakfast, his phone rang, making him drop his fork to the plate with a clatter. "Hello?"

"Just thought you might want those lab results." The lab tech's grin was almost audible as he waited for the tension to build, for Jason to prompt him out of frustration.

"They're done already? Wow. So? Give."

"Well, there were indeed elements of sand in that piece of glass you gave me. In fact, most of the elements of it are exactly the same as glass: Silica, carbon..."

"Get on with it." Jason scowled impatiently.

"Okay. The really strange thing is this: Embedded in the glass were some very strange fibers. They were part organic and part inorganic. But their properties would make them highly conductive, as in electrical impulses. They were almost like artificially produced neurons of some sort."

"Any idea how they got there? What might have produced them?"

"Not a clue. But I'll tell you one thing. Whatever left them there was alive at some point in time."

"Anything else strange?"

"Isn't that enough?"

He blinked several times, then grinned condescendingly.

"Yes, I suppose it is. Listen, I'm going to text you a phone number. It's for the sheriff's department down in Florida. They're investigating the case that I pulled this evidence from. Can you send a copy of the report over to them? It might help."

"You bet. You want me to email you a copy too?"

"That'd be great. Thanks, man."

He cut off the call, feeling suddenly inspired and confused.

Moments later, he breezed into his office and dropped into the chair, propping his feet up on the desk for good measure. Smiling, he dialed Trina's number from his recent calls list and waited for her to pick up.

"I just had a really interesting talk with the lab technician who ran the sample I gave him."

"Hello to you, too, Jason." She giggled into the phone. It evoked images of sleepovers, pillow fights and first kisses. "And? What was it?"

"It's not so much what it is, as what it is not."

"All right, then. What isn't it?"

"It's not glass. At least not plain old ordinary glass. It has little fibers embedded in it which are part organic and part inorganic."

"And...?"

"And they are highly conductive, like neurons. As if something alive had at one time passed through or over the glass."

"And you find that strange." Trina sounded hopeful, amused.

"Hell, yes. Don't you?"

"Well, yes and no. Follow me on this, Jason. What if something were living inside Brenda Walsh. Using her as a sort of host. Eventually, the host body would wear out and it would have to relocate. So, it found ample opportunity with Chloe. But Chloe fought back and Brenda died before the transfer could be made. So, the thing...whatever it is...managed to get to Chloe's then-deceased body and enter it. Wouldn't that account for her sudden reanimation? And the seemingly instant repair of her injuries? Maybe even the change in her eye color."

"Yes, Trina, but what would that thing be? An alien? A spirit? What?"

"I don't know. Nothing shows up on any of her tests."

"She's not exhibiting any of the symptoms that Brenda would have had."

"Maybe it's too soon." She screwed up her face as she thought about this. His silence told her that he was trying to rebuke her theory. "I think we have to go back to Ft. Myers. I think we have to talk to Chloe again."

"On what basis? That we have weird glass?"

"No. On the basis that there's some strange entity running around and taking control of people's minds."

Jason laughed out loud at this, not particularly caring if he offended her or not. "You really are a lunatic, you know that, Trina?"

"Yea, but I'm a fun lunatic. What do you say, Jason? Road trip?"

"Sure! I don't have anything better to do than drive back and forth to Florida." A headache was coming on, hard and fast.

"Awesome! Go pack."

The two of them left for Ft. Myers the same day. As luck would have it, they were able to get their old rooms back at the Best Western. It was the off-season in Florida, so rooms and rental cars were a dime a dozen.

As a courtesy, they notified Sheriff Barnes that they were back in town. Then, they enjoyed a quiet dinner and a night of vacuous television.

Chapter Three

Jason was sleeping soundly in his motel room when he suddenly got the impression that he was not alone. In his dream, he was seated on the chair next to the requisite motel-room desk when someone's shadow fell over him. Before he could turn around to see who was there, he awoke, sitting bolt upright in his bed and panting with terror. He wasn't sure if his stark fear had been brought about by the dream, or whether some real external force had conjured it.

He was in the middle of talking himself down – and doing a pretty poor job of it – when he sensed someone standing on the other side of the room. He whipped his head around so that he was staring directly at the form, then his panic blossomed once more as he recognized the intruder.

"Chloe! How did you..." He made as if to stand up, then found that his legs simply would not withstand the strain. They buckled and he collapsed onto the bed once more.

"Ssh! Please don't tell anyone you saw me. I need your help, Mr. Callahan. You're the only one who understands. You're the only one who can stop it."

"Stop it? Stop what, Chloe?"

She buried her face in her hands and began to sob softly, the tears trickling out from between her fingers and soaking her cotton hospital gown. This time, Jason made a more concerted effort to stand, meeting with some success and actually managing to propel himself forward a few steps.

In a flash, Chloe was gone, her atoms disbursing like so much chimney smoke on a windy day. Jason stopped in his tracks, frozen there by fear and the anticipation of her return.

After several moments of stagnation, he finally admitted that Chloe would not be coming back.

He staggered to the phone and hastily dialed the number of Gulf Coast Hospital. A groggy voice responded to the ring and Jason cleared his throat loudly before speaking.

"Second floor nurse's station, please."

"This is Nurse Adams. What can I do for you?"

"This is Jason Callahan. I was in before with Sheriff Barnes. I know this is going to sound crazy, but could you go check and make sure that Chloe Marsh is still in her room. I'll wait."

Nurse Adams hesitated a moment, obviously torn between hanging up on a prank caller and pissing off a private investigator. "Just a moment. I'll check."

After what seemed an eternity, Nurse Adams picked up the line once more. "Yes. Chloe's still in her bed."

"Are you sure? Did you actually see her face?" He knew that he sounded like a lunatic. At this particular point in time, he didn't much care.

"I saw her face. There's no doubt about it. That's Chloe."

"Thank you." Jason placed the phone back on its cradle in slow motion, wondering all the while just what he had seen in his room.

The vision was far too detailed to have been a dream. The clarity of it was what had frightened him most. He could hear that little ring in her voice and could actually see the familiar pattern in the fabric of her hospital gown.

He wondered what he should do next. Should he go to visit Chloe and risk being thought a fool or a madman? Or should he just keep the whole incident to himself? He decided on the latter.

He crawled back into the bed and pulled the covers up under his chin. No matter how many of these things he had dealt with and no matter how he tried to talk himself into not being afraid, the simple fact of the matter was that he just couldn't bring himself to turn out the light.

He laid there for some time, his eyes inexorably drawn to that one corner of the room where Chloe had appeared to him. He was finally made to admit that, if he did not turn out the light, he would lay there for the rest of the night, staring at that one barren point in the room. He finally screwed up his courage and switched the light off, spending another sleepless hour staring blindly into the darkness in the fear that she would return.

Jason trudged into the motel dining room that morning, looking like death warmed over. Trina was already there, hunched over a cup of coffee and skimming the morning paper. She looked up just in time to see Jason take his seat and her eyes scanned his rumpled form.

"What happened to you? You look like you haven't slept a wink."

"That's because I haven't." He leaned over in the direction of the waitress and placed a hand on her arm. "Could I get a cup of coffee when you get a chance?" He managed a smile for her as she moved off in the direction of the kitchen.

"So, what kept you up last night? Lumpy mattress?" Trina smirked at him over the rim of her cup.

"I had the single weirdest dream of my life. At least I think it was a dream."

Trina noted the befuddled, almost fearful look in his eyes. "Jason, what was it?"

"Well, I was lying there, asleep in my bed. And all of a sudden, I woke up feeling like there was somebody in the room with me. When I looked over at the corner, Chloe was standing there. She was still wearing her hospital gown and she kept asking me to help her. She said I was the only one who could save her. Then, she started crying and when I took a few steps toward her, she just disappeared into thin air."

Trina looked at him for a long beat, confused by how much this dream had rattled him. "Well, Jason, I can imagine how unsettling it must have been, but I don't think it's all that bizarre given the circumstances. I mean, you're here investigating a strange death involving a woman who just happens to make a practice of dying and coming back to life. It's only natural that it would be on your mind. Your subconscious was just playing tricks on you."

"But Trina, I'd swear I was awake. I mean, the whole thing was so vivid. More vivid than anything I've ever experienced. I was so convinced that Chloe had really been in my room that I called the hospital to make sure she was still there."

"And was she?"

"The nurse said she was sound asleep in her hospital bed."

"There you have it. You were dreaming. Nothing more." She smiled, placating him and hoping he wouldn't see through her. That smile faded the more she thought about the incident. "Unless…"

The waitress poured his coffee, then readied her pad to take their breakfast orders. Jason had just opened his mouth when his phone rang, jangling his already unsteady nerves.

"Callahan."

"Oh, Mr. Callahan! I'm so sorry to bother you. This is Chloe Marsh. Dawg gave me your number."

"What is it, Chloe? What's wrong?" His eyes met Trina's, though only briefly.

"Could you come over to the hospital? Now? Please?" Her voice was so unsteady, so high-pitched with fear that it set Jason's teeth on edge.

"Well, sure. Maybe if you'd tell me what's wrong…"

"I can't talk about it over the phone. Please. You're the only one who might understand. The only one who might help."

"We'll be there in a flash." He shoved the phone into his pocket and placed his napkin on the table.

"What's up, Jason?"

"Chloe wants us to come to the hospital. She sounds pretty upset."

"Okay. Let's go."

She followed him out of the small restaurant, wondering just how much stock he was still placing in this dream. She had an inkling what had happened but she wasn't going to tell Jason that. It would freak him out too much.

Since his eyes seemed hardly able to focus, Trina drove the short distance to the hospital. Judging by the quiet at the nurse's station when they arrived, no one else had any idea that something was amiss.

"Oh, thank God you've come," Chloe gasped as they entered her room. She looked even paler than before; her hands twisting and folding the edge of the sheet.

"Chloe, this is my partner, Trina Dane. Trina, this is Chloe Marsh."

"Hi," Trina said with a smile, settling into the chair next to the bed and studying the girl. She watched her carefully, noting the color of her aura, the odd sort of vibration which came from her.

"Is everything okay, Chloe?" Jason asked her as he sat on the edge of the vacant bed.

"I don't really know any way to explain it to you. I'll just have to show you." She checked his face, trying to judge just how much this demonstration might frighten him. Then, she pressed on. "Keep your eye on that book over there on the chair."

Jason and Trina's eyes traveled to the hefty volume which now lay on the green vinyl chair across the room. At first, they saw nothing whatever out of the ordinary. Then, the book began to slowly levitate off the chair, traveling through the air at an increasing rate of speed until it reached Chloe's waiting hands.

She turned her sullen eyes on Jason's incredulous face. "See what I mean? And that's not all. Watch the water glass."

She made the water glass levitate off the table a few inches. Then, she made the bathroom door open and shut and the TV change channels. When she had finally completed her show, she looked at him again, her eyes pleading.

"How is it that I can do that? How can I make it stop?"

Jason found the whole thing staggering. He looked to Trina, then back to Chloe. "I could be wrong, but I think you're demonstrating some sort of psychic power. Has anything like this ever happened to you before?"

"Never. And I don't want it to be happening now."

"When did this start?" Trina inquired.

"Just this morning. I got bored with TV, so I thought I'd read. Only the book was over there on the chair. So, I just thought about how nice it would be if the book came to me, so I wouldn't have to bother the nurse. And it did." She was still wringing the edge of the sheet, her knuckles white with the effort.

Trina leaned forward and placed a reassuring hand on the girl's arm. "It could be due to your head injury. It's not common, but I've heard of people developing sudden psychic abilities after a head injury or…a near death. Have you spoken to Dr. Walker about this?"

"Heavens no! I don't want people to think I'm weird." Her voice had gone up an octave and her face had paled.

"Well, I think it would be a good idea if we did tell him about it and maybe he can run some more tests. Maybe something will show up that they missed before."

"Miss Dane, have you ever seen anything like this before?"

She thought about this for a moment before answering, then decided on the more diplomatic approach. "I've seen some cases of psychic abilities where people were able to move objects with just their mind. But they usually were born to it. We'll talk to Dr. Walker about getting some tests done. We'll know more then."

"It's probably just a side-effect of your injuries," Jason offered with a wink. "It'll probably go away on its own in a couple of days."

That seemed to calm her somewhat, though she still hadn't found her smile. Trina followed Jason into the hall, taking care to shut the door before they spoke.

"Do you really think it'll go away, Trina?"

"No," she said flatly, turning to the nurse's station. "Excuse me, nurse? Could you tell me where Dr. Walker is, please?"

The nurse beamed at Jason and smoothed back her blond hair. "He's in the lounge at the moment. Down the hall, last door on your left."

"Thanks." Trina flashed her a sarcastic smile and walked to the end of the corridor, then pushed open the heavy wood door.

Jason stepped in ahead of Trina, then closed the door softly behind them. "Dr. Walker could we have a word with you?"

The doctor stood quickly, leaning to look into the doorway. "Ah, Mr. Callahan. What brings you back here?"

"Actually, Chloe called me about an hour ago. Did she say

anything to you about having any trouble?"

"Trouble? What kind of trouble?" His eyebrows had knit themselves together over his nose, giving him an appearance that was more menacing than concerned.

Jason sank heavily into the chair across from Walker and let go of his breath. "She seems to be experiencing some sort of psychic episode. She's able to move things across the room, that sort of thing."

Walker's eyes were on the verge of rolling out of his head. "As far as I'm concerned, such things don't exist outside of science fiction. And now, here it is, right in my own hospital. You've witnessed this?"

"We both did," Trina interjected, stepping nearer to the men.

"What could cause such a thing? Her near-death experience maybe?" Jason's face was a mask, all boyish charm gone, replaced with worry.

"I wouldn't call it 'near-death'. If anything, it was pure death. But that might be one explanation. Many people who have crossed over to the other side have returned bearing certain gifts, for lack of a better term. And Chloe was there for more than just a brief visit." Trina nodded resolutely and proffered a smile.

The silence nearly smothered them all. Then Walker cleared his throat and turned his eyes to Trina. "And you are?"

"I'm sorry." Jason tried to smile, found his face inept. "This is my associate, Trina Dane."

Trina thrust out one hand, bracelets and rings dancing, jangling as she gifted the doctor with that mega-watt smile of hers. "Pleased to meet you, Doctor."

He shook her hand, though he wiped his own palm on the legs of his pants when he was through. "And I take it you know a thing or two about psychic phenomena?"

"Miss Dane is here because she's the world's leading expert on such things."

Dr. Walker regarded Jason as though he was the fabled White Rabbit and had just hopped across his path. "Indeed."

"And because I have to tell you that your little nurse friend, Liz, isn't coming today. And that your wife knows." Trina cocked her head to one side and grinned.

Dr. Walker paled at that. He blustered and bellowed and finally let his eyes settle on the floor, avoiding Trina's gaze as he spoke. "Well, I wouldn't want to get behind any paranormal explanations until we've ruled out all the scientific ones. I think we should order an EEG and a follow-up CAT scan right away."

"I agree completely," Jason chimed in, silencing Trina with one glare while the words were fresh on her tongue.

"All right, then. We'll do it right away. You can be there if you like."

Trina nodded her agreement. "We should go tell Chloe."

The corridor, which really only stretched twenty feet from end to end, seemed unbelievably long just then. The three of them marched down the hall, their feet tapping lightly on the linoleum as they went. Apparently, Chloe had heard them approaching, and she used her newly acquired talents to open the door for them. Walker hesitated momentarily, eyeing the door warily as though it might at any moment slam in his face.

"Good news, Chloe," Jason began.

"Yes, I know. You've decided to run some more tests on me."

Jason shot a glance at Trina, whose raised brows only hinted at how stunned she was. "How did you know that?"

"I overheard you talking."

"But you couldn't have heard us," Walker disagreed. "We were at the other end of the hall with two closed doors between us."

"I heard everything you said. You're going to give me an EEG and another CAT scan."

"That's impossible. You couldn't have heard that."

"I'm sorry to disappoint you, Dr. Walker, but I did hear it. You said that as far as you were concerned, such things didn't exist outside of science fiction. And now here it is right in your own hospital."

Walker was frozen where he stood. Jason looked at Chloe with something akin to pride. She was returning his gaze, though she seemed intent on something else.

"I didn't read your minds, Mr. Callahan. I heard you quite clearly."

All the color drained from Jason's face as he turned toward Trina and Walker. "That's just what I was thinking. I was thinking that she must have read our minds somehow." He looked back in Chloe's direction, only to see the beginnings of tears.

"Then it's true? I did hear your thoughts?"

"It's all right, Chloe. Don't panic." Walker stepped over to the bed, his hand hovering just above her shoulder, though he couldn't quite bring himself to actually touch her. "There's got to be some logical explanation for this. Mr. Callahan and Miss Dane are going to come with us while we do those tests. Then we'll know for sure what's causing this."

"And how to get rid of it?" Her eyes begged for the proper response.

"Probably."

She allowed them to load her into a wheelchair and take her downstairs for the tests. Her face remained fixed throughout the procedure, refusing to betray either fear or worry. Jason and Trina watched through the little window as she held perfectly still for the CAT scan, then they walked beside her all the way to the EEG room.

"Now, this isn't going to hurt. We're just going to put some probes on your head so we can see what your brain waves look like." The technician had a serene smile, her eyes continuing the theme.

Chloe held still as she put the little sensors all over her head, then crossed her arms across her chest impatiently. Jason stood at her side, looking at her in wonder and trying not to have any thoughts which might frighten her if she picked up on them.

"I'm going to take a base-line reading first," the technician advised, adjusting her equipment. "Then, I'm going to ask you to do a couple of things for me so I can see what happens. Okay?"

"Sure," she sighed, staring at the ceiling and frowning.

"All right, now. I want you to close the door for me." She waited patiently for what she thought would be a no-show, then nearly fled the room as the door began to shut. "That was...uh... very good, Chloe. Try something else."

"You can't wait for Friday. You leave on your vacation on Friday. To Hawaii, right?" She spared not a glance for anyone else in the room, but kept her eyes trained on the ceiling.

"That's right," the technician murmured, feeling a rash of goose bumps travel across her entire body. She looked down at the machine and bit contemplatively into her lip.

"That should be all we need. Thanks." The technician stepped in to remove the sensors from Chloe's head. She seemed hesitant to touch Chloe; anxious to get away from her.

Chloe sat up and stared at them, one by one. "So, what's going on?"

"Well, your EEG base lines are completely normal," the technician offered. "But when you shut the door and read my mind, your alpha waves went right off the scale. And a completely different band shows up."

"What does all that mean?" Chloe had the innocent eyes of a very young child. Those eyes now looked as though they belonged to a war-weary octogenarian.

"It means that your brain is somehow able to operate on a level that most people don't even have."

"So, what's causing it?"

Dr. Walker rounded the corner, bearing Chloe's scans and a wide smile. He slid them onto the lighted screen and motioned for Jason and Trina to join him.

"If you'll look right here, you'll notice a small...growth, for want of a better term. You know as well as I do that it wasn't there yesterday. But it's there now. It's not a tumor. And it's not a hemorrhage. Have either of you ever seen anything like it?"

Trina leaned in close to Dr. Walker and whispered. "No. It looks like..."

"Yes, I know." He shared a knowing glance at her, then turned his eyes back to the x-rays.

"Would you like to clue us in?" Jason requested impatiently.

"Well, it has all the properties and tissue density of...of a..." Walker broke off, not really brave enough to give voice to the truth.

"What?" Chloe barked, her eyes wide with anticipation. "What does it look like?"

Trina turned around, her face stoic and unreadable. "It looks like another brain."

Chloe fainted.

Jason was standing next to Chloe's bed when she started to come around. Her head lolled from one side to the other, her eyes barely fluttering. When her lids finally did peel back, she found it hard to focus her eyes on anything at all. She licked her lips and swallowed hard, wincing at the dryness of her throat.

"Here," Jason offered, "let me get you some water."

He pivoted to reach for the pitcher, only to see that Chloe had beaten him to the punch. The pitcher was suspended in mid-air, filling the cup of its own volition. The straw lifted off from the table and docked with the cup en route. He watched, fascinated, as the girl drank greedily from the cup, then returned it to its former resting place.

"What's happening to me, Mr. Callahan?" she slurred hoarsely, her mouth somehow not obeying her brain's commands.

"I'm not exactly sure, Chloe. But I don't think it's anything you should be afraid of." He had lied in that last, though he intended nothing more than to soothe her jangled nerves.

"Just make it stop. Please."

Trina moved in with a smile and a wet wash cloth. She mopped the beads of sweat from Chloe's forehead and tried on a smile. "Tell me, when you were with Brenda that night, did you see anything strange?"

"You mean, other than Brenda?"

"Yes. Other than Brenda."

"I didn't have time to see anything else. I was too busy fighting her off."

"You didn't see anyone else? Perhaps a strange cloud or a puff of smoke?"

She looked at Trina's face, confused by her odd questions. "Nothing. Should I have?"

"I don't know. I'm just trying to find some way of explaining what's happened to you."

Dr. Walker stepped through the door just then, his cheerful

expression masking his stark fear of the girl. "How are we feeling?"

"I don't know about you, Dr. Walker, but I'm feeling damned strange. Pardon my French." She blushed at that, a nice girl using such profanity.

"Well, we've given you a mild sedative to help you get some rest."

"Whatever this thing inside my head is, can't you just take it out?"

"That's just the trouble. We don't know what it is, so we don't know if it would be safe to remove it. Any kind of brain surgery is risky and we don't want to put you in any danger."

"I don't care. I'd rather be dead than be like this." She turned her head toward the window and fought the flood of tears which was even now welling up behind her lids.

"Why don't we let her get some more rest. We can't do any more today."

Jason looked at the back of her head, feeling such sympathy for her that it threatened to overwhelm him. "You know where to reach me if you need me."

"Thank you," she said in a small, tremulous voice.

Walker held the door for Jason and Trina to walk past, then shut it quietly. "I've called in a friend of mine from college. A Dr. Canton. He's the leading brain man in the country. I'd feel a whole lot better knowing he was here. Just in case."

"That's a good idea," Jason said. "I've got a couple of things to take care of. All right if I come back this evening and check in on Chloe?"

"Sure. She doesn't have a whole lot of people left around here. I'm sure she'd be glad to see you."

Jason shuffled slowly down the hall, his body and his mind feeling the brunt of the stress. He wanted to take a nap but he felt so over-tired that he doubted sleep would come that easily.

They went first to the motel, where Trina went straight to the Internet, trying to find anything that might even remotely resemble Chloe's case. Jason threw himself on the bed, one arm over his eyes, hoping that sleep would somehow come to claim him.

"Did anybody get the number of that truck? I feel like hell," he mumbled

"That happens when you don't sleep for extended periods of time."

He struggled to a sitting position and stretched mightily. "So, are you finding anything?" he yawned.

"A couple of very interesting things. First of all, there was a death very similar to Brenda's about two months ago in Tampa. As coincidence would have it, Brenda just happened to be in Tampa for a convention on that very same day. And she was booked at the same hotel that the deceased stayed at."

Jason suddenly felt very alert. "Go on, Trina. You have my undivided attention."

"Three months prior to that, there was a similar death in Baton Rouge. This time, a used car salesman."

"Well, no accounting for taste."

"Two months before that, a postal worker in Kansas. Two months before that, a doctor in LA."

"Whatever it is, it's heading east."

"It?" she questioned snidely, turning to meet his gaze.

"Yes, it. Whatever. Let me ask you something, Trina. Remember that sample I took from the road where Brenda died? Is there any mention of something like that in any of the other cases?"

"Not that I've seen. But that doesn't mean there wasn't. Jason, what are you thinking?"

"I'm thinking I need to take a vacation." He collapsed on the bed then, rubbing his temples and shutting his eyes. "No, seriously. I'm wondering if there's a pattern to these deaths. Something they all had in common. Some genetic trait, a certain predisposition to it."

"Something like...say...they were all victims of a car crash or they were all the same race?"

"Yea, something like that. Maybe this thing needs a particular type of metabolism. Or it avoids people with diabetes. Something along those lines. Am I making any sense, Trina?"

"More than a little. There's a thing involved – an entity, if you will – and it needs specific bodies or types of bodies to survive." Trina thought for a moment. The act contorted her face and drew the color from it. "It can't be just a disembodied spirit, though. No ordinary one, at least. It must be something stronger, more malevolent. Like a demon or an ancient."

"Ordinarily, I'd say you're nuts. But considering Chloe's strange resurrection and her new-found psychic abilities, I'd have to say there's at least a remote chance that you're right. But where did it come from? I suppose we can check into these other deaths, try to uncover some sort of pattern. But what does it want?"

"To survive. That's all any sentient being really wants. And if it needs a host body to accomplish that, then it will do whatever it has to to get one."

"It might explain the rapid healing of Chloe's body. Maybe even the return of her appendix and tonsils. But what about the growth in her head? What purpose might that serve?"

"Do I look like Mr. Wizard to you? I don't have all the answers. Just some." Trina's color had returned. It brought with it a smile. "I'll get some names and addresses off the computer. We can check these people out later. Right now, what you need is some rest."

"Bless you, Trina." He sank back onto the bed and curled himself into a fetal position.

"Not here, Jason. Go back to your own room."

"And they say the Maytag repairman's lonely." He reluctantly got off the bed and padded back to his own room.

He had been worried that Chloe might pay him another uninvited visit, but his poor mind and body were so tired that he slipped into a dreamless sleep the second his head hit the pillow. At around six, the phone rang, scaring the life out of him and making him smack his head smartly on the headboard.

"Yes," he panted into the receiver, his eyes stuck open from the fright.

"Mr. Callahan? This is Sheriff Barnes. I think you better get down to the hospital right away. All hell's breaking loose and you might be the only one who can calm her down."

"You mean, Chloe?"

"Yeah. Hurry."

"On the way."

He dove into his clothes while he alerted Trina, his head filled with sleep-induced cotton and most of his body numb. He met her in the hallway and trotted to the car as he filled her in on what little he knew.

They arrived at the hospital only minutes later. The hallway was filled with people, huddled together and whispering quietly among themselves. A small cluster of nurses had gathered together at the desk, clutching at each other in panic. Outside of Chloe's door, Sheriff Barnes stood guard, his back pressed tightly to it and one beefy hand grasping the knob.

"What's going on in there?" Jason asked as the din reached his ears.

"See for yourself." Barnes stepped aside and as he released the knob, the door flew inward with a crash.

Jason dared to look inside, where some unseen force appeared to be wreaking havoc on the hospital furniture. As he took one wary step inside, he spotted Chloe, her knees drawn up to her chest and clutching her head with both arms. She was moaning softly and crying, her whole body shaking with the effort of...what?

She turned her swollen eyes toward him then. They were red and haunted and it made Jason cringe just to look at them. Still, he shored up his strength and took another bold step toward her.

"Oh, God! Make it stop! Please. I'm not doing this. How do I make it stop?"

The drawers on the bureau were crashing open and shut. Small objects were flying about the room, hurling themselves at the walls. Her bed was banging up and down on the floor as she bounced about. Both windows were shattered. And in the midst of it all was Chloe, terrified, helpless Chloe. She had no understanding of how or why all this was occurring and her eyes told the whole story.

Trina ran to her at once and grabbed her by both shoulders. "Look at me, Chloe." She failed to respond to Trina at all, so she shook her once, gently. "Look at me. Look right into my eyes and nowhere else."

She did as Trina asked, her eyes still filled with tears and panic. They softened mildly as they gazed into Trina's.

"Do you trust me, Chloe? Do you?"

"Yes."

"All right then. You can control this."

"No, I can't."

"You can," she affirmed sharply. "You just have to calm down. Nobody's going to hurt you. I won't let them. Take a deep breath." Trina watched as she followed her instructions. "Hold it. Good. Now, let it out slowly. Just relax. Take another deep breath."

Trina glanced hurriedly about the room, noting that things had calmed down slightly, though the room still seemed to have a life of its own.

"And let it out slowly. Okay, now I want you to lay back. There's nothing to be scared of. I'm here to protect you. Close your eyes and take another deep breath."

Trina cast a look back over her shoulder at the others, who were still frozen in terror.

"That's great, Chloe. Do you feel my hand in yours?"

"Yes."

"All right. When you start feeling afraid or uptight, you just squeeze my hand. But remember, there's nothing here that's going to hurt you."

She slowly allowed her eyes to open and locked them on Trina's. A tear trickled slowly down her cheek, making its way to the pillow. "What happened?"

"You just lost control, that's all. This is all so new to you. You just have to learn how to work it." Trina stroked her forehead tenderly and graced her with an endearing smile. "Feeling better now?"

"Much." She tried on a smile. It fit.

"Can you tell me how this all started?" Trina eased onto the edge of the bed, all the while maintaining possession of her hand.

"I had a bad dream. I dreamed that somebody else was

inside my body. I was outside it somehow. And my own body was chasing me, trying to kill me. When I woke up, everything was going crazy, flying around and stuff." She started to tremble again and so she squeezed Trina's hand roughly.

Trina smiled in the face of the pain, intent on keeping her calm. "I think it would be a good idea if you let Dr. Walker give you something to help you sleep."

She nodded her agreement and bit into her lip. "Will you stay until I fall asleep?"

"Sure." She waved Dr. Walker and Jason into the room, keeping eye contact with Chloe. She managed to keep a smile on her face while Dr. Walker gave Chloe the injection, stroking her hand for good measure. Chloe was still shaking a bit and her color hadn't returned. "I'm going to step outside to have a word with my partner. I'll be right back."

Trina slowly stood up, keeping a watchful eye on Chloe. When she gained the hall, she pulled Jason, Walker and Barnes aside.

"I think it would be safer if we kept her sedated until we know what's causing this."

"That's a wonderful idea, Miss Dane," Walker sighed. "Truth is, we have to keep increasing the amount of sedatives each time. She's developing an amazing resistance to them. I don't know how much longer we can keep putting her under."

"If we can't keep her under control, we're going to have to remove her from the hospital." Barnes frowned, clearly not wanting to jeopardize Chloe in any way, but knowing where his priorities lie.

"Sheriff Barnes, surely you don't intend to just put her out on the street?" Jason's tone was dry, hard at the edges, and threatening at its core.

"Mr. Callahan, I don't see any other choice. There's no end to the damage that girl can do. I love Chloe as much as anybody, but there's no telling who might get hurt if she gets out of control again."

Jason sighed resignedly and eyed Trina. "Well, I'll stay here tonight just in case something happens."

"That's a good idea, Mr. Callahan. She seems mighty sweet on you."

Jason exhaled loudly and stalked back to Chloe's room, where he pulled a chair to her bedside and eased into it. "How do you feel, Chloe?"

"Like a turtle with two shells."

"Huh?" He snickered, a happy relief for his sagging spirits.

"I'm so danged tired that I feel like a turtle toting around two shells." She met his eyes, offering up a smile of her own.

"Ah!" he said, tilting back his head and chuckling some more.

She lay on her side, gazing at him with increasingly unfocused eyes. She forced a smile for him, then licked her lips lethargically. "So, does Mr. Callahan have a first name?"

He smirked and shifted uneasily in his seat.

"What's the matter? Did your parents name you something weird like Horatio?"

"Nothing that awful. My name is Jason."

"Jason. I like that. It really suits you. Jason Callahan, P.I. Good name for a TV show, if you ask me." She eyed him peculiarly, wondering if she would have the courage or the strength left to ask what she needed to. "Jason, I want you to promise me one thing."

"What's that, Chloe?" He rubbed her hand instinctively.

"If things get worse, if I start hurting people, I don't want you to worry about me. What I mean to say is, it's more important that I not hurt other people than it is that I don't get hurt. If push comes to shove, you do what you have to do. Even if that means killing me. Okay?"

He studied her face for a long time, suddenly impressed by how wondrously beautiful she was. Her beauty wasn't in the turn of a leg or the artful placement of a cheek bone. The beauty of Chloe was in the simple goodness of her heart, the story in her eyes.

"It won't come to that."

"But if it does..."

"I will take measures equal and appropriate to the threat presented. Good enough?" Ah, cop lingo. It never failed. He smiled even though his heart was breaking.

"Good enough."

"Good. Now go to sleep."

She did.

Chapter Four

Jason awakened the next morning, still crammed into the green chair and stiff as a board. He could hardly move his head at first and his back cried out in protest as he moved to sit up. He had fully intended to go back to the motel once Chloe had fallen asleep, but his mind hadn't had the good sense to get his body moving in time.

He looked in Chloe's direction and was made aware of the fact that she was staring at him. He wondered if she was reading his thoughts; if she had read them last night.

"Good morning," he moaned, embarrassed at being seen in such a disheveled, unprofessional state.

"I didn't expect you to spend the whole night, you know. You could have gone back to your motel."

"I didn't expect to, either. I guess I was just a little too tired to make the move." He scrubbed one hand across his bristly chin and stifled a yawn.

"Well, you're going to be suffering for it all day long." She reached out and touched his arm affectionately, drawing both their eyes to it as their flesh began to heat up. "What was that?" she queried, drawing her hand back.

Jason straightened, one hand on his formerly aching back and one on the bed. "I don't know but my back sure feels better."

She gaped at him in confusion. "Did I do that?"

"You just might have. Is there no end to your talents?"

She smiled, happy that she had finally done something helpful rather than harmful. "I did that. I just healed you." She giggled like a child and – if Jason didn't imagine it – she kicked her feet with joy.

"You sure did." He chuckled then, smiling in spite of himself.

"You should go back to the motel now, Jason. I've taken advantage of your kind heart quite enough. And I feel so much better. Honest, I do."

"If you need me, don't hesitate to call."

"Sure thing, Jason." She took pleasure at how disconcerted he was by that simple familiarity. He was genuine and kind. She liked him very much.

Jason went back to the motel, where Trina was just dressing for the day. He knocked on her door, then leaned against the wall in complete exhaustion. When she opened the door, he glared at her through sleepy eyes.

"Jason! What on earth happened to you?"

"I spent the night scrunched up in a chair," he mumbled as he staggered past her. "How about you?"

"Slept like a baby. How's Chloe?"

"Better than yesterday. How did you make out on those other deaths?"

"Well, I spent a good bit of time gathering all the information I could about the victims. So far as I can tell, they had absolutely nothing in common. They're not related in any way. In fact, only two of them shared the same blood type. They have different occupations, different income brackets. As far as I can tell, they were just chosen at random."

"Oh well. I guess we're back to square one." He dropped onto the chair by the window, the springs of the chair groaning in protest.

"Not entirely. There are a few options. But hear me out before you interrupt."

"Don't I always?"

"No," she stated flatly.

"You're right. Go ahead. I promise not to interrupt."

"If this were a straight on demonic possession, I would recommend an exorcism. But a straight-up demonic possession wouldn't require the possessing demon to physically move from host to host. It wouldn't leave evidence, if you catch my drift."

"Go on." He had lived through enough of Trina's stories to know that she would reach her point eventually. Any derailment on his part would just make her start over again.

"Okay, so we have to be dealing with some sort of disembodied spirit…"

"I thought you said it couldn't be that."

"No ordinary disembodied spirit. This has to be an ancient one. It's been around for ages and it's very powerful. It has the strength to not only affect the body it inhabits, but its surroundings as well. And that makes it just about the most powerful entity there is."

"So, how do we get rid of it?"

"I don't know." She paused there, her face worried, without guile. "I sent an email to an old friend of mine. He's in Columbia on a dig right now, so we might not get an answer right away. I don't have any rituals or spells that will drive out something like this. It would just laugh at anything I've got."

"So, what do we do until your friend gets back to you? And don't say 'pray' because that's a cop-out and you know it."

"I think the important thing now is to find something that disagrees with this entity that still won't hurt Chloe. Something physical. You know, drive it out of her."

"And into what?"

"I don't know. We'll have to place her in an isolation ward of some sort. Wear decontamination suits and the like. Although, God knows exactly how this thing transfers. A decon suit might not make a bit of difference."

"Well, while I was sleeping it off over at the hospital, you were coming up with a plan. I like that about you, Trina."

"Thanks. Right now, I think you should go back to your room and take a shower."

"Smells like a good idea."

Jason awakened to a frantic rapping at his door. When he finally achieved a vertical position and made it to the door, Trina was facing him down with urgency and fear.

"Come on, Jason. We've got to get to the hospital."

He yawned loudly and rubbed his face. "What's wrong?"

"Dr. Walker just called. There's been a fire at the hospital. It started in Chloe's room."

Jason grabbed his clothes off the back of the chair and ran into the bathroom. "Did he say anything else?" he hollered from the other side of the door.

"No. Just that we should come down there right away."

"Let's go," he sighed, snatching up his phone as he breezed past the chair.

Once they arrived at the hospital, they spotted the center of activity at once. Several fire trucks had gathered just outside the emergency entrance. Firemen were milling around casually, speaking into radios and wiping soot from their faces.

"Jason Callahan, P.I. What's happened here?"

"I'm not exactly sure, sir. A small fire broke out on the second floor. It could have been a lot worse, but I think we have it under control now."

"Any idea what caused it?"

"Not yet. We're still investigating."

Jason and Trina left the man to his duties and continued their trek to Chloe's room. When the elevator doors slid open on the second floor, the stench of smoke was everywhere. Jason coughed twice, then stepped onto the linoleum tiles. Dr. Walker was standing next to a gurney in the hallway, his back to them.

"Dr. Walker, what happened? Is Chloe all right?"

Walker turned to meet them, his face having aged ten years since their last meeting. On the gurney sat a terrified and smoke-blackened Chloe, her eyes the single lightest part of her body. "We're still not real clear on what happened, Mr. Callahan. The fire seems to have started in Chloe's room, though I can't say just how."

"I told you," she coughed. "It was me."

"How could it be you, Chloe?" Jason stepped closer, unsettled by her wild appearance but still concerned about her state of mind.

"I was asleep, having this dream. In the dream, I was very cold, like you might get if you were stranded for a long time at the Arctic or something. And in my dream, I gathered up some firewood and started a fire. When I woke up, there was smoke everywhere and the bed was on fire."

"You weren't hurt, were you?"

"Weirdest thing," Walker offered. "She doesn't seem to have been touched at all, even though most of the bed burned up around her."

"I inhaled some smoke is all. How could I have done this, Jason? How?" She looked near tears; near hysteria.

"I don't know," he mumbled, placing one steadying hand on her shoulder. It came away covered in soot.

Dr. Walker drew one hand over his face, leaving a streak of black char down one cheek and across his chin. "Well, we can't have her staying in the hospital any longer. We've had to evacuate the whole floor as it is. No telling what might happen next time."

"You can't just send her home," Trina admonished, her eyes more fraught with anger than fear.

"We can't keep her here."

"But..."

"The doc's right, ma'am." Sheriff Barnes had come up behind them, his hands customarily thrust into his pockets and his face grim. "We do have to consider the safety of the other patients."

"It's all right. I don't mind. They don't seem to be able to help me much here anyway." Chloe blinked and sighed, scrunching up in a tight little ball as she watched the goings-on in the hallway.

Trina evaluated Chloe's sincerity in this. The girl was brave, no doubt about that. But she was also terribly frightened and, for the most part, helpless against whatever power seemed to be controlling her thoughts.

"Well, we're not going to let you stay alone. If anything happened, there'd be no one there to help you. Jason and I will stay with you."

She looked up at Trina, her eyes brimming with tears again in the unvoiced fear that something else was probably going to happen – and soon. "I appreciate that. I do. But I don't want..."

"Is it all right if we take her home now?" Jason asked, cutting Chloe off before she could talk them both out of it.

"No reason why not. For all intents and purposes, the girl's perfectly healthy."

Jason fetched a wheelchair from the nurses' station and gestured wildly at it. "Hop on. I'll give you a lift to the car, if you're not afraid of my driving."

She smiled a bit at that, reminding herself to thank the Lord for such friends as Jason and Trina.

Jason drove them to Chloe's apartment, a smallish, two-story building only two miles down the road. Though it was by no stretch of the imagination posh, it was tasteful and cozy. Jason took a look around, amazed at the sheer number of plants that were in the place.

"How long have you lived here, Chloe?"

"About two years. As soon as they put this development up, I came to have a look at it. I fell in love with it instantly because of the fact that every apartment had its own patio or balcony."

He nodded in agreement, relaxing a bit, though the threat of Chloe's strange abilities still hung over him.

"I have a twin bed in the guest room and a sofa bed out here. You two can divide who sleeps where. There's always clean sheets on the bed and I'll put out some fresh bath towels."

"Don't go to any trouble on our account," Trina called as she disappeared down the short hall, Jason in tow. "We're very easy to please." She waited until she was sure Chloe couldn't hear them, then she leaned close to Jason. "Do you think we should tell Chloe what we suspect she's up against?"

Before Jason could reply, Chloe called to them from down the hall. "I think you should always be honest with Chloe. She's not a child, you know."

Trina grimaced, feeling instantly stupid for having forgotten Chloe's new-found psychic abilities. It gave her a new appreciation for what Jason dealt with whenever they worked together.

"Now, Trina. I'll make us some tea and then we can all sit down and discuss this thing of yours."

They watched her warily as she set about preparing the tea. She was far too at ease with all this, far too accepting. It might have been because she had long ago touched upon the theories trickling through their minds. Jason didn't think so. He thought that somehow, some way, this thing that had control over Chloe was getting stronger, was taking even more of her power away from her. The simple fact was, they had no way of knowing exactly who was in control of Chloe. For all they knew, the thing inside of her had been in control since she had died out there on that road.

"There, some nice herbal tea. It should calm us all down." She set the tray on the table before them and filled three cups. "Sorry there's no milk. Well, that's not exactly true. There is milk, but it's rather chunky at the moment." She smiled wanly, then sipped her tea.

"Chloe, we don't want to scare you any more than you already have been. We just think you need to know what you're up against."

"It's all right, Trina. I think at this point any more fear would be superfluous. I've already been scared just about as bad as a person can be."

Jason and Trina exchanged worried glances, shocked at the girl's use of such a word. "Chloe, from everything that we've been able to gather, we think you're dealing with something that's...well...let's just call it extra-natural."

"I'll buy that, Jason. But just what exactly is it, this extra-natural thing?"

Jason swallowed hard, fearing that, no matter how he approached it, he would come off sounding like some sort of raving madman. "Judging by the sudden appearance of such strong psychic powers, and the burnt track of sand on the road where Brenda died, we're inclined to believe that something was living inside of Brenda..."

"And now it's in me. What is it?" She said it with such decisiveness, such calm resolution that it frightened Jason even more.

Trina sat up straight; looked directly at her. "I'm not exactly sure. It could be merely the spirit..."

"A ghost?"

"Something like that. Or perhaps an alien presence."

She snickered mockingly. "Oh, please. I've never been

abducted by aliens. I've never even seen a UFO."

Trina shook her head. "I didn't imply that you had. I'm just saying..."

"The thing that's growing in my head, could that be it?"

"Whatever is growing in your head is more likely to be a by-product of that entity," Jason corrected, trying to maintain a clinical detachment in the face of Trina's zeal and Chloe's almost blasé attitude.

"So, why not just take it out?" She sipped some more tea, then set the cup on the table for fear that the rattling of cup against saucer would betray her true emotions.

Trina watched this woman, who above all was simplistic in her points of view and virtually without pretense, change faces before her very eyes. She was at one moment, the uncomplicated, sweet Chloe whom they had come to know. The next, she appeared to be a wiser, nearly deceitful woman who not only accepted what was happening to her but condoned it. Trina straightened visibly and chose her words carefully, not wanting to frighten Chloe or to threaten whatever might be in possession of her mind at that particular moment.

"We don't really know what that growth is. I feel it's safer to try and find a non-invasive solution. We might be able to find something which would drive the thing out of you." She watched Chloe's face for changes, signs that it was not really Chloe who was hearing her words.

"Brenda died with it still in her. Either she didn't react the same way, or she didn't have enough time to get help. I don't want to go like that. It's not that I'm afraid of dying, exactly. Right now, that seems like a much better choice than going on like this. But, if I die, what will become of this thing?"

Trina remained silent for a moment, not wanting to be that truthful with Chloe. In the end, she realized that there really was no secret capable of being kept from her. "It will probably try to go into somebody else."

"If there's nobody else around?"

"I don't know," Trina said softly, her eyes averted, hands clutching her cup tightly.

Jason took over again, trying to be gently and at the same

time itching to dig at Chloe for any fragment of information that he could get. "We just don't know enough about this thing to be able to tell you anything for certain. Maybe you could think of something that might help."

"Such as?"

"I don't know. Did you feel anything when this thing entered your body? Or maybe you're getting some kind of sensation from it?"

Chloe studied his eyes, thinking this over but coming up empty. "I'm sorry. I was unconscious when it all happened. Dead, really. And I don't have the sense that anything's in here with me."

"All right, I think we're all a little tired just now. I suggest we try to get some sleep and in the morning, we'll discuss what sort of therapy we might try to get this thing to leave you."

Chloe nodded slowly, her eyes staring across the room at nothing in particular. She stood at once, picking up the tray and returning it to the kitchen.

"If you need anything, be sure and let me know." Chloe walked to the hallway and then turned back. "I really do appreciate all you're doing to help me. I don't know anybody who would go through all this for someone they don't even know."

With that, she was gone, into her room and into a deep sleep.

Jason turned himself so that he was facing Trina. His face was haggard, his hair disheveled. "Trina, do you have any idea what this thing is?"

"Not a clue. But whatever it is, it's old. Really old. And very strong. I can sense its presence. I can't read Chloe or it. But I know it's here."

"Do you have any idea what will get rid of it? Is there anything?"

She wanted to tell him she did. But she couldn't lie to him. "I've never run up against anything like this, Jason. I'm going to call some friends tomorrow. Perhaps one of them will have heard of it. Or maybe they at least have an idea what will drive it away. For now, I think we should get some sleep. Tomorrow is apt to be a mighty tough day."

"Do you want bacon or sausage?" Chloe asked them across the breakfast bar which separated her kitchen from the living room.

Jason was refolding the sofa bed and he cast his response over his shoulder. "Bacon would be fine."

"You don't have to cook for us, Chloe," Trina added, climbing onto one of the wicker bar stools.

"Nonsense. Mama always said that a happy guest will be a frequent guest. I feed anybody who comes into my home. Even stray cats."

"Could I possibly get another cup of coffee?" Jason asked sheepishly, hesitant to get under foot in the small kitchen.

Chloe turned on him with a broad smile, one hand on her hip and the other wielding a spatula. "Mama had another saying. I'll get you the first one. After that, you're family and you can get it yourself."

"Yes, ma'am," he blurted, offering a mock salute.

Chloe was in high spirits that morning, almost as though nothing untoward had happened to her. She was maddeningly warm and charming and she had that sort of natural innocence that just seemed to suck a person in. It was hard to believe that that sweet girl harbored a malevolent spirit of some sort.

She served them breakfast: Heaping stacks of pancakes and bacon with a side of hash browns. Jason and Trina took one bite and mistook her apartment for heaven. Chloe smiled knowingly, stuffing her own mouth as she watched them eat.

"You sure are a good cook," Trina marveled.

"Hey, Trina. Maybe you could take some lessons."

Trina poked Jason roughly in the ribs and scowled at him. "As soon as I have someone to cook for, I will."

They ate in blissful peace. Nothing extraordinary had happened during the remainder of the night and, from all outward appearances, nothing ever would again. Chloe seemed to be back to her innocent, light-hearted self. They knew enough to avoid that sort of false security, but as long as the moment lasted, they would enjoy it to its fullest.

Chloe cleaned up the breakfast dishes, shoving them into

the dishwasher and switching it on. Then, she sat down in her official TV-watching recliner and pierced Jason and Trina with her eyes.

"So, why don't you tell me what your plan is?" She was smiling rather purposefully now, her expression seeming almost rehearsed.

"To begin with, I'd like to go out to LA and have a talk with the family of that doctor." Jason's hands worked idly at the hem of his polo shirt as he spoke.

"What doctor, Jason?" Chloe questioned, her eyebrows rising automatically.

"We've found three other deaths similar to Brenda's. The first was a doctor in LA. I'd like to go out and talk to his family. See if I can learn anything."

"Oh."

"And while he's gone, we can get started on your treatment." Trina smiled and winked at her, hoping the mood wouldn't deteriorate. "But first, humor me. Take a drink of this." She produced a small, ornate crystal bottle and removed the stopper, holding it out to Chloe with a bright smile.

"What is it?" Slowly, Chloe's hand closed around the bottle, holding it delicately as though it might burst.

"Holy water. Just humor me."

Chloe checked her face for signs of deceit, shrugged and took a long drink from the bottle. Wiping her mouth with the back of one hand, she passed the bottle back to Trina. "Now what?"

Trina cast a sideways glance at Jason and shook her head. "Nothing." Then her smile was back. "Okay, now we can discuss treatment."

"What have you decided, Trina?"

She turned toward Jason and drew in a deep breath. "Well, to begin with, I think we should try the most innocuous treatment first. We really don't know anything about what's causing your problems, Chloe, or what it might react to. Something as simple as an aspirin might be enough to kill it. Or, it might be something radical. So, we'll start with some antibiotics and anti-viral medications. Then, if that doesn't work, we can move into the more radical treatments."

"Radical?" Chloe pushed the recliner into an upright position, poised for bad news, her face fading at the mere prospect of some horrible medical treatments. "You mean, stuff like chemo or radiation?"

"Something like that." Trina nodded, keeping her smile firmly in place.

"But what if it's something simple, like too much chocolate or something?"

"Well, we know it's not bothered by cholesterol," Jason quipped. "Judging by your diet, you must have the highest cholesterol of any living person."

"Have you given any thought to where this thing's going to go if it does leave me?" Chloe's face looked more worried by the minute. She had aged since the whole thing began and it showed.

Trina shifted uneasily in her seat and shared a tense glance with Jason. "Presumably, it's going to go into the nearest available body."

"Which would be you, Trina." Her mouth fell open, working feverishly but producing no sound. Her eyes were filled with panic as she swallowed back the hard lump of terror and found her voice once more. "I don't want anybody to get hurt because of me. Especially not you."

"That's why, at least as far as the drug therapy goes, I'm going to be taking the same doses as you."

"And that'll work?"

"I don't know. But it's the best idea I could come up with. Without knowing what we're dealing with, we really have to try anything and everything. And that means everything from exorcism to drug therapy, if need be. If we have to move on to such things as radiation, we'll move you to a facility where we can place you in a sealed isolation room."

"You sure you'll both be okay alone here?" Jason wanted to know.

"We'll be fine. Won't we, Chloe?" Trina smiled and rubbed the girl's back lightly.

"Sure. Fine." She was sitting, entranced, and gave no sign of recognition when Jason spoke to her.

"I'm going to schedule the first available flight to LA. With any luck, I'll be back tomorrow. Okay, Chloe? Chloe?"

Her eyes snapped back into focus and she feigned a smile for him. "Okay, Jason."

He went into the kitchen to use the phone, leaving Chloe and Trina to their own devices. "As soon as we drive Jason to the airport, I'd like to talk to a friend of mine. He'll be able to get us everything we need. And he can be on call if we need him."

Chloe nodded idly, her mind focused on other things.

The two women drove Jason to the airport and watched through the expanse of glass as his plane took off. That was when the first tentacles of fear began to wind themselves around Trina's mind. When she turned to leave, she was sure that her face held none of the confidence and solace that she had intended. "Shall we get started?"

"Why not?" A smile flashed across Chloe's face and then it was gone. "How are you going to get the things you need? You're not a doctor or something, are you?"

"No, I'm not a doctor. But I know a guy." Trina cast a wink in her general direction, then started for the car.

"Well, I know that Jason's a detective. But what is it that you do? Are you some sort of shrink or something?"

"Actually, I'm just a psychic. I write a column for the *Times.* But that's just my day job. What I really do is deal in things that are outside the realms of...normality."

"You mean, ghosts and stuff like that?"

"Yeah. Ghosts, demons, voodoo curses, shape-shifters... like that." She climbed in and started the car, waiting for Chloe to fasten her seatbelt before she put the car in gear.

The two drove to a nearby strip-mall on the east side of town. It looked for all the world as though it had been abandoned. The only sign of life was a small light shining through the limo-black film on the front window. A huge depiction of the planet Earth graced the front window; that and nothing more. Trina pulled open the door and it exhaled incense and herbs. Behind the tiled counter stood a short, thin man, folded over a book and smoking a cigarette. He looked up as they entered his shop, confused by the sudden appearance of customers.

"Why, hello, ladies. How are you today?" He put down the book and straightened, his eyes drawn to Chloe and stuck there.

"I'm Trina Dane. I believe Calvin spoke to you about me." She extended one jangling hand and smiled.

"Ah, yes." Instead of taking her hand, the man took a step backward, his face paling a bit as he looked back and forth between the two women. "Which one of you has the hitchhiker?"

"That would be me," Chloe chimed in, trying to smile. Her face just wasn't up to it.

The man had grown steadily more pale as the conversation had drawn on. Now, he began to mumble under his breath and he pulled a small bag from beneath his shirt and held it tightly in his fist. "Do you know what it is? Who it is?"

"Not a clue," Trina sighed. "And so I'll be needing a few things."

"Such as?"

"I'm just visiting here, so…everything. Black candles, white candles, some goofer dust, a few crystals…"

"Here," he said, sliding a pad and pen across the counter to her. "Write it all down and I'll get it for you."

Trina turned the pad and began to scribble furiously on the paper. "Before it's all said and done, I will probably need a doctor who knows how to keep his mouth shut."

The man regarded her with something akin to awe and nodded slowly. He still hadn't released the bag from his hand. "I have someone I work with. We've all needed him from time to time."

"Awesome. I appreciate it." Trina gifted him with a smile and batted her eyes.

"Her aura is black." He said it flatly, as though he were making a declaration about the weather.

"Yes, I know." She turned to Chloe and gave her what she hoped was a reassuring smile. "It happens sometimes."

The man lowered his eyes to the paper and began to shake his head slowly. "You sure you know what you're doing?"

Trina leaned over the counter, her expression not quite threatening but her jaw set and her gaze firm. "Sweetie, I've been doing this since before you were a glimmer in the Goddess's eye."

He glanced over Trina's shoulder to Chloe, then looked back to Trina again. "I'll get these items for you. It'll take just a minute."

Trina composed herself, straightened her smile and turned back to Chloe. "See? Everything's going to be just fine, hon." She rubbed Chloe's arm reassuringly. "Just fine."

But of course, it wasn't.

Presently, the little man came out of the back room, a box in his arms, and in that box were the items Trina had asked for. He set it down on the counter and sighed, stepping out from behind it so he could see Trina's face. "I had most of the items you listed. But no way in hell can I get ahold of a Hand of Glory. You want that, you'll have to make one."

Trina cocked one hip to the side and screwed up her face. "Damn. Well, I'll just have to go another way. You did have the antibiotics and anti-virals, right?"

"Yep. He looked rather uncomfortable as he met Trina's eyes once more, though he tried hard to conceal that fact. "Fifty units BID? That's an awful long course."

"I'll be taking it, too. When and if that thing leaves her, I'd like to be as distasteful a target as possible."

"I see." He began adding up the prices, then paused, pen in mid-air. "Chloe, how do you feel about this?"

She perked up then, her face losing a bit of color and her eyes darkening. "How did you know my name?"

He offered his first smile. It made his face even more boy-like. "The same way Miss Dane did." He tapped his head and winked.

Chloe nodded and smiled. "I'm all for anything that'll get rid of this thing."

"I still can't believe this is happening right here in our own small town. I mean, it's all just so...bizarre."

"I've seen stranger things. Things you'd never believe."

He eyed Trina for a moment, finding that he had come to like this woman very much over the past few minutes. "I'll just bet you have, Miss Dane."

She took the box from him and offered her hand. "Thank you. You've been a great help to us."

"Anything I can do. You have my home number. Don't hesitate to use it if you need help."

"Thank you," Chloe offered with a smile.

As they left the shop, Trina nudged Chloe with one shoulder. "I say we rent a few movies, go home, put our feet up and relax."

"Hooray for that! This is going to work. I just know it is."

"Are you always this optimistic?"

"So, what am I going to do? Sit around and convince myself that nothing's going to make this go away? Tell myself that my life is over? That I'll die a horrible death in just a few short days or weeks? What good would that do? Mama always said that sorrow only breeds more sorrow."

"Your mother was a very smart woman."

"Yeah. She had me, didn't she?" Chloe smirked playfully at her, then began to swagger haughtily as she walked toward the car.

"Down the hatch," Trina said, holding forth one of the pills and a glass of water.

"Over the teeth and past the gums, look out tummy, here it comes." Chloe took the pill and tossed it into her mouth, then drained the water glass.

"Now, let's watch that movie." Trina dropped onto the sofa and picked up the remote.

Chloe sat down beside her, propping her feet on the small coffee table and grinning. "Gee, I wish we had some popcorn."

Like a bolt of lightning, a huge red ceramic bowl appeared on her lap, brimming with hot popcorn. Chloe looked at Trina with something akin to mischief, then winked.

"Well, it may be scary, but at least it has its benefits." She took a piece and crunched on it for a moment, then held the bowl out to Trina.

"No thanks. It gives me the creeps."

"Aw, come on. It's perfectly all right. Taste it. It's delicious."

"No way."

"What are you? Chicken?"

Trina began to cluck like a chicken and then they both burst into peals of laughter. If there were anything at all lurking in the shadows, it sure didn't show in their faces.

Once the movie was over, Trina got ready to retire. She had pretty well settled herself into the spare room and Chloe had actually gotten quite used to having someone else around all the time. She had lived alone for so long, that she had nearly forgotten how nice it was to have someone near.

Chloe had some trouble dropping off to sleep. Since beginning her therapy, Chloe had spent nearly every waking second obsessed with whether or not it would work. She worried about when and where the thing would leave her; waited tensely for it to happen. And so, she lay in her bed, staring at the darkness and listening to silence. She wondered what it would feel like, what it would look like and if she would be alive at the end of it.

Shortly after midnight, she did manage to slip into sleep. Trina had been having a dream, to which Chloe had made herself privy. She watched the woman's mental pictures roll by like a feature film, astonished at how clear it was and yet how surreal it felt. She knew that this was a horrific invasion of her privacy, but she simply couldn't stop it. More and more, she found that her mental calisthenics were more reflex and less effort.

Chloe awoke the next morning to the sound of the shower running. Momentarily, she had forgotten the fact that she no longer lived alone and so the unbidden sound startled her awake. As she padded out into the hall, she finally realized that her roommate was the source of the sound and so she turned to go back to bed despite the late hour.

Trina came out of the bathroom just as Chloe reached her bedroom door. Her eyes were drawn at once to the muddy footprints upon the beige carpet and then to Chloe's besotted feet.

"What have you been up to, Chloe? Gardening in your bare feet?"

Chloe looked at her as if she had just sprouted horns. "What are you talking..." Her eyes traveled down her form to her feet, then stuck there. "Oh, my gosh! What's happened to me?"

"Have you ever had problems with sleepwalking?"

"Not that I've been told. I haven't left the house since yesterday. I swear. At least, I don't remember going out." Her eyes were swimming in fear as she at last looked up at Trina once more.

"Well, we'll figure this out later. Right now, you ought to go in and take a shower. Don't worry about the carpet. I'll clean that up."

Chloe had a mind to protest, then thought better of it. Mechanically, she plodded into the bathroom, where steam still laced the mirror. "Trina? Where do you suppose I went?"

"I don't know, Chloe. But I think we should find out."

Chapter Five

Jason walked up the steps of the two-story Spanish Colonial house and checked the name on the door. "Dr. and Mrs. Reed Warren," the plaque read. As he rang the bell, he mentally crossed his fingers, hoping that Mrs. Warren would be able to provide some smidgen of information that would help him.

A lovely woman of about fifty opened the door, her red hair done into a tight French twist and her pretty face smiling at him. "May I help you?"

"I'm Jason Callahan. I'm a private investigator. I know this is an inconvenience, but I was wondering if I could ask you a few questions regarding your husband's death."

She stared back at him for a moment, her face expressionless, leaving Jason with the mounting fear that she would simply send him away. "Come in," she offered simply, standing aside so that he could pass.

Her lips were tightly pressed and she watched Jason with more than casual interest as he walked past her and into the hallway. "Please excuse the state of the place. My maid is on vacation and...well...I'm not very good at these things."

The house was immaculate. Every stick of antique furniture in the place looked as though it had been polished just that morning and the wood floors gleamed up at him. Mrs. Warren led him into the expansive living room, which was dominated by an enormous gothic-looking fireplace.

"Now, what would you like to ask me, Mr. ..." She raised her brows in that cultured, questioning way that true ladies sometimes do.

"Callahan, ma'am. I hope this isn't too painful for you."

"Not at all. I've had quite some time to mourn and I think I've come to grips with it."

He offered a conciliatory smile, then looked at his notes. "This is in regard to a case I'm working on in Florida. I've been able to link your husband's death with four others like it across the country. I was wondering, did he show any signs of illness over the past few months before his death?"

"Not a one until the very day he died. He woke up feeling rather feverish and nauseous. He stayed in bed all that morning but then he forced himself to go into the hospital anyway. That's the way Reed was. Duty at all costs. He seemed very agitated anyway, like he just couldn't make himself sit still for a second. The last time I saw him was when he kissed me good-bye as he was leaving. Two hours later, a policeman came to my door to tell me that he was dead." She swallowed hard and fussed about with her hand in her lap.

"What did they list as the cause of death?" He already knew the answer. He just wanted to get at any suspicions she might have.

"Heart failure. They said his heart was extremely enlarged."

"And what do you think?"

She eyed him curiously for a moment, trying to get a feel for what he was getting at. "I just don't know. He's very careful about getting his check-ups and the sort. And he's never had any trouble with his heart at all. Besides that, there's the odd way in which he died."

"How's that?"

"Well..." It was clear from her tone and her hesitation that she was reluctant to release this little tidbit of information. "On the way to the hospital, he suddenly just swerved his car up onto the sidewalk in front of a restaurant. He walked right inside and approached a woman who was dining there. As far as I can tell, he had never met this woman before. That notwithstanding, he simply grabbed her and kissed her, right there in front of God and everyone. Then, he simply collapsed onto the floor...dead."

"This woman, did you ever get her name?"

"A Mildred Kendall. From Kansas. She was apparently here on vacation with her family."

Jason looked deep into her eyes, sizing up her ability to handle what he felt he had to tell her. "Mrs. Warren, Mildred Kendall died some months later under similarly peculiar circumstances and from a heart attack. Three days prior to her death, she drove herself to the emergency room, complaining of aberrant behavior and a high fever."

"Oh. My." She sat straight as a board, her face suddenly slipping into that practiced, complacent mask.

"Before she died, Mrs. Kendall apparently had a very strange encounter with a Miss Barbara Morgan, who later also died from the same type of condition."

"My heavens! This is starting to sound like one of those odd little virus movies they're so fond of making these days. Are you suggesting...?"

"I'm trying to find the cause, Mrs. Warren, not suggest one. We have a young woman in Florida who now suffers from the same kind of malady as your husband. We're trying to help her before it's too late."

"I am very sorry to hear that. I'm afraid I don't know anything that might help, though I can give you the name of a gentleman who might know a great deal more than I about this thing. He was a patient of my husband's. He called me a few weeks after Reed died and said that he wanted to meet with me. He said he had information about Reed's death that I might want to know. I never did meet the man because, frankly, I was just too weary to deal with it. Besides, nothing he could possibly tell me would bring Reed back. His name is Professor Donald Stillman. He's an archaeologist at UCLA. This is his number." She passed a business card to Jason, then watched his face carefully.

"You just happened to have his card sitting on your coffee table?"

"He stops by almost once a week to ring the bell and, when I don't answer, he leaves one of his cards in the mailbox. He used to call every day, but I had the number changed." She studied her hands, gracefully perched in her lap, for a moment, then raised her soft blue eyes to meet his. "Mr. Callahan, whatever might or might not have happened to my husband, I'd really rather not know about it. I do wish that woman well. Honestly, I do. I just can't deal with dredging up all that pain again."

"I understand, Mrs. Warren. And I thank you for taking time to speak with me."

He strode out of the house with Mrs. Warren hot on his heels. She was a pleasant enough woman but Jason got the distinct impression that she was not all she appeared to be. Perhaps she was hiding something mysterious about her husband's death. Perhaps she simply had another man in her life and was not anxious to have the world find out about it. In either event, he would leave the woman to whatever devices got her through the night.

He went back to the hotel and immediately called Professor Stillman's office. They informed him that the man was on a dig in Columbia and would return the next day. Disappointed, Jason decided that he would call Trina and fill her in. He would also have to tell her that he would stay on in LA, for one more day. He was sure that she wouldn't be thrilled about it but there was simply no other way.

All through breakfast, Trina kept eyeing Chloe suspiciously. Where had the girl gone last night? And what had she done? The very thought that Chloe could disappear from the apartment like that without arousing her scared Trina beyond words. She would feel so much better if Jason would just come back.

Chloe was doing dishes when the phone rang. She wiped her hands haphazardly on her apron and then grabbed up the cordless phone.

"Hello?"

"Hi, Chloe, darlin'. How ya doin' this morning'?" It was Sheriff Barnes, though his usually sunny tone had a ring of deception to it.

"I'm feeling okay, I guess."

"Could I talk to that Mr. Callahan of yours?" On the other end of the phone, Barnes voice cracked.

"He's not here. He went out to California on an errand." She felt obliged to tell him no more than that.

"Did Miss Dane go with him? If not, I'd like to speak to her."

"Just a moment." She passed the phone over the breakfast bar to Trina. "It's Dawg."

"Sheriff Barnes. What can I do for you?" She was confused by his call, more so by the fact that he had asked to speak to her rather than Chloe.

"I don't want you to make like anything's going on. Just keep a good poker face and we'll be just fine."

"Okay." She scanned Chloe's face, hoping against hope that she couldn't read her thoughts just now.

"Last night, around three, someone broke into the hospital's pharmacy and stole some drugs."

"What kind of drugs?" Again, she checked Chloe's expression for signs of comprehension.

"Pain killers, sleeping pills, downers mostly. A lot of them." He paused for a moment, listening to the frightened silence between them. "Here's the reason I asked to speak to you first. I wanted to ask you if Chloe was at the apartment all night."

Trina turned her back on Chloe, somehow feeling as though direct eye contact might increase the chances that she would read her mind. "No."

"I understand you can't talk with Chloe right there. And, really, I understand the trouble Chloe's having. I don't want to do anything that might upset her at this point."

"Yes." She began fidgeting nervously with her robe, picking at the chenille and partially denuding it.

"The thing is, the silent alarm in the pharmacy was tripped when the culprit broke the window on the door. Two of their security guards showed up and actually caught the thief in the act. One of them was badly injured when the perpetrator threw him twelve feet down the hall and into a glass door. The other fired one shot into the perp, directly into the chest. Miss Dane, the perpetrator was Chloe."

Trina straightened, feeling the first tingle of icy fear trickle down her back. She turned a wary eye to Chloe, who seemed not in the least bit interest in the conversation. "Are you sure?"

"I wouldn't be calling you if I wasn't. One of the security guards remembered her from her stay here. Described her to a tee. And we have her on the security video. Miss Dane, you said that Chloe wasn't in the apartment all last night. Since you can't very well talk, I'm going to lob a few at you and you just see if you can return them. Okay?"

"Yes."

"She did leave at some point during the night, didn't she?"

"Yes."

"Do you know what time?"

"No. I went to bed around eleven, so I must have missed it."

"Ah. And you never saw her come back home?"

"No. I got up around seven."

"Gotcha. Well, is there anything else you can tell me?"

"Yes. Footprints." She spun her head then, feeling Chloe's eyes burning into the back of her head.

"I see. Well, this is one fine kettle of fish we got here. On the one hand, I'm obliged to put the guilty person behind bars. On the other, I can't very well punish Chloe for something she had no say in. I'm gonna talk it over with the hospital administrator and see if I can't get him to cut her some slack, being that she's... of diminished capacity and all."

"That's a good idea. And I'll see what I can find out for you. Good-bye, Sheriff Barnes."

She passed the phone back to Chloe, who seemed nonplused by the whole affair. Then, she sat dolefully on one of the barstools, watching Chloe clean the white tiled counters and hum.

"Dawg called about me, didn't he?" Chloe stated out of the blue.

Trina met her eyes reluctantly, then sighed in resignation. "Yes, he did, Chloe."

"It has something to do with where I went last night."

"I'm afraid so." She watched as Chloe slowly made her way around the counter and took up a position on the stool next to Trina's. "I don't want you to get upset over this."

"Why don't you just tell me what it is? I'll get it out of you eventually anyway." Her eyes were so demanding, so piercing that it made Trina cringe inwardly.

"All right. It seems that someone broke into the hospital

pharmacy last night and stole some drugs. They also injured one of the security guards who tried to stop them. He managed to produce a perfect description of you, along with your name. And you show upon the security video."

Chloe's hands were trembling now, tightly knitted together and resting on the counter. She bit into her lower lip and scowled at her hands, knowing what everyone else only suspected.

"So, sometime last night I slipped out of the apartment and robbed the pharmacy. I don't remember leaving, but I woke up with mud all over my feet." Her voice began to tremble even more now, running a close second to her hands. "And the guard says it was me. So, it must be me."

"There's one more thing, Chloe." She swallowed hard and drew in a deep breath. "One of the security guards claims to have shot you in the chest."

Chloe looked momentarily confused, as if Trina were speaking a foreign language. Then, slowly, she pulled open her robe, exposing the top third of her chest. There, just below her breast bone, was a raised, deep red circle of skin. It looked as though it was flesh, reddened and growing over something, and the longer Trina stared at it, the more it seemed to be moving, still growing.

"Then it really was me."

Trina looked into her tragic, guilt-pained eyes and wanted to cry. "All the evidence points to you, yes. But if there's one thing I've learned in my years investigating such things, it's that evidence can be and often is deceiving. Let's look at this logically. If you did indeed go there and steal some drugs, then they must be here somewhere. Right?"

Chloe brightened a bit at that last, feeling one single ray of sunshine creep into the dark corners of her soul. "Yes. Where else would I take them?"

"Then, why don't we just go have a look, huh?" Trina managed a tenuous grin for her, sliding off the stool and offering her hand to help Chloe down from hers.

Hand in hand, the two women went first to the bathroom, where their search turned up nothing out of the ordinary. Next, they rummaged through the hall closet and then Chloe's own, still finding nothing. Chloe was beginning to take heart in the fact that they could find no evidence when Trina dropped to her knees and began searching through the things under Chloe's bed.

"Uh-oh," she murmured, pausing in her search before extracting herself from under the bed. When she sat up, she held in her hand a large plastic bag containing several dozen medication bottles.

"Oh, God!" Chloe sobbed, collapsing limply on the bed and burying her face in her hands. "It was me. It really was. I don't remember ever leaving here last night. And I don't remember ever seeing those bottles. But I did it. I went there. And I hurt that man. How could I do all those things and not even remember it? How?"

Trina crept onto the bed beside her and wrapped one anchoring arm around her heaving shoulders. "Calm down, Chloe. The guard wasn't hurt too badly. You didn't kill anyone..."

Her eyes shot to Trina's, searching them, reading them. Hysteria took hold and Chloe's breath came in huge gulps. Her body trembling even more now, she began to lose control. "Yes, but how long before I do? How long before I kill someone? How long before I do something really monstrous? How long, Trina?"

"You've got to get hold of yourself, Chloe. This isn't going to help anyone."

She shot to her feet, staring down at Trina as though from a million miles away. "What was I going to do with these? Was I going to kill myself? Or was I going to kill someone else? What would I need with all those drugs? What would *it* need with them? I couldn't stand it if I hurt anyone. Especially not you. You've got to get those out of here right now. Before I...*it*...uses them. Get rid of them. And check all the food. Check and make sure I didn't poison the food. Or the milk. You can't trust me anymore. You can't trust me not to hurt you."

Trina grabbed her by the shoulders and shook her hard. "Stop it! You're not responsible for this. Or anything else this thing does with your body. It's just using you and you don't have any control over it."

She pushed herself off from Trina in one swift movement. "But I should. Don't you understand? I should have control over my own body, my own actions. But I don't. This thing is turning me into a monster, Trina. And nothing you or me or anybody else can do is gonna stop it."

She bolted out of the room and ran, shrieking, down the hall to the bathroom. Once inside, she slammed the door hard and locked it, collapsing against it in wretched sobs.

Trina followed, worried that she might try to hurt herself. Thanks to the recent search of the bathroom, she knew that there were no sharp objects in the room, no medication stronger than Tylenol. She knocked on the door and called to Chloe, but nothing she did would elicit a response from the devastated girl. Then the phone rang again.

Trina ran to the kitchen and pawed the phone roughly off its cradle. "Yes?"

"Trina, you sound out of breath. Is everything okay there?" Now Jason's tone was nearly as frantic as her own.

"Actually, things here are a bit...hectic."

"How so?"

"It seems that Chloe left the apartment last night, without waking me or her, for that matter. She broke into the hospital pharmacy, stole a considerable amount of medication and then roughed up a security guard for good measure. And all without having any knowledge of it."

Jason whistled through his teeth and cleared his throat. "I'm almost finished here so I'll be taking the afternoon flight out."

"That's good news. I could use some help." She paused, trying in vain to catch her breath. "So, were you able to get anything useful while you were out there?"

"If you call pneumonia useful. Whoever it was that said it never rains in southern California should be shot. It hasn't stopped raining since I got here."

"But were they any help? Did you get any information?"

"Some very good information. The wife of the doctor says that he was fine right up until the day he died. Then, he seemed to run a very high fever. He had trouble concentrating and was extremely agitated. As she put it, he couldn't sit still for a second. About noon, he decided that he needed to go to the hospital anyway to do his rounds. Before he got there, he stopped his car on the sidewalk in front of a Mexican restaurant and went inside. This is where the really weird part starts. He just walked in, took a look around, then went up to a couple who were seated at a table in the back of the room. He grabbed the wife by the shoulders and kissed her for no reason at all. Then, he just dropped dead."

"Wow! That's even stranger than Brenda Walsh's attack on Chloe."

"I did a little digging with the LAPD. And Trina? The woman he kissed was the same woman from Kansas who died almost three months later."

"So, the thing made its transfer when he kissed her. Have you been able to dig up any relationship between the woman in Kansas and the case in Baton Rouge?"

"Not yet, though I'm pretty positive one exists. I did, however, get the name of a Professor Donald Stillman, a patient of the doctor's whose wife died under similar circumstances and whose son nearly died. He contacted Mrs. Warren after the death of her husband and said that he had something to tell her about how her husband died. She never got back in touch with him because she was just too distraught to talk about it. The man's an archaeologist associated with UCLA. He's gone on a dig but he's expected home today. Since you're having so much trouble there, I figure we could call him together and see what he has to say."

"Jason, Professor Stillman is the friend I emailed about this whole thing. He's an expert in ancient religions and cults. What's more, he knows more about ancient spirits and possession than any person alive."

"What are the odds that we would be put in contact with the same person? I don't mind telling you, I'm severely creeped out right now."

"Well, in spite of all that, you've certainly put together a lot of the pieces."

"So, how's Chloe holding up?"

Trina spared a parting glance at the bathroom door, then stepped fully into the kitchen where she would be less likely to be overheard. "At the moment, she's not doing too well. As you can imagine, this whole incident with the pharmacy has taken its toll on her. And I don't think the therapy's doing much good. I think it would be a good idea to step it up as much as possible. Try something a little more aggressive."

"Hopefully, Professor Stillman will be able to tell us something that might help. I'll be leaving soon, Trina, so hold down the fort until I get there."

"I'll defend it to the last drop of your blood."

She placed the receiver back in its cradle, then returned her attentions to the bathroom door. Where there once had been agonized sobs, there was now only silence. That, more than the sound of hysteria, frightened her.

She tapped lightly on the door, biting into her lip and praying that Chloe was still all right. "Chloe? Honey, are you all right?"

"Yes," came the weak, sniffling reply.

"I've got good news. If you come out, we can talk about it."

She waited outside the door, hearing the soft, muffled sounds of Chloe blowing her nose and then the click of the door lock disengaging. Chloe's face, when it appeared in the doorway, was tortured, swollen. Her eyes wavered between anger and sadness so that Trina never could get a really good fix on the girl's state of mind.

"Come sit down with me. We'll talk."

She followed Trina to the sofa, then slumped onto it in despair. "I'm listening."

"I know you're listening, Chloe. But you've got to really hear me. Okay?"

"Okay," she groaned, playing the part of the belligerent child now, her lips pouty and her eyes mocking.

"I just spoke with Jason on the phone. He's coming back this evening."

"Did he learn anything?"

"Yes, he did. He spoke to the wife of one of the other victims. She described her husband's death as being very much like Brenda's. Which certainly means that we're dealing with the same thing here. She also gave him the name of a man who seems to know a great deal more about this thing than the rest of us. I guess he might be the closest thing to an expert we're ever going to get."

"So, he knows what it is? How to stop it?" Her eyes looked cheerful, hopeful, though only for an instant.

"We're not sure yet. He's out of the country right now. But he's coming back today and Jason and I will speak to him. We'll find out everything he knows and maybe then we'll be able to stop this thing."

She sighed resignedly, sinking even further into the sofa and staring at the floor. "Hurry up and wait. Hurry up and wait. What are we gonna do in the meantime?"

"For starters, we're going to step up your therapy. I'd like us to start taking an anti-viral medication. And if that doesn't work, we're going to move you to the hospital in Tampa. They have a large, secured isolation ward there. We can put you there while we try a less conventional approach. That way, we won't risk this thing getting away from us."

"You mean, like an exorcism or something?"

"Something along those lines, yeah." She smiled briefly, but all hint of it faded fast. If there was one thing she hated more than anything else, it was the casting out of evil spirits. It never ended well.

Chloe turned her sullen eyes on Trina, scarring her with her sorrow. "You'll stay with me, though? You won't just leave me there?"

"Of course. Jason and I will both be at the hospital with you."

"That's good. I don't want to die alone."

Jason walked off the plane looking for all the world as though he had just been on a two-week bender. His face was cleanly shaven but his eyes were dark and sunken and his clothes looked as though they had been slept in. He forced a smile for Chloe's sake, though he didn't feel that there was much of anything to smile about.

It was dark outside and hot. The humid air clung to everything it touched to the point of being heavy against one's body. Jason paused to wipe a trickle of sweat from his brow, then walked up to Trina.

"How are we doing? Okay?"

"Better." Trina looked fondly at Chloe, whose spirits seemed to have lifted immeasurably since Jason's arrival.

"What's say we stop someplace and get something to eat on the way back to the apartment. I'm sure Chloe's tired of cooking for us."

"Oh, no, Jason. I never get tired of cooking."

"Be that as it may, we've got a nice expense account and the bosses get worried if we don't use it enough. Come on. Admit it. Couldn't you use some good Italian food or maybe even some good Mexican?" He grabbed her about the shoulders and gave her a playful little shake.

"When did we get an expense account?" Trina asked suspiciously. "Or bosses, for that matter?"

"Didn't I tell you? I spoke to the family of the lady in Kansas. They agreed to foot the entire bill in order to find out what happened to her. So, Chloe, what do you say to that dinner?"

She pretended to think this over for a moment, then snapped on her internal lamp. "There is a great Italian place just up the road a piece. I think I could survive gorging myself on some lasagna."

"There you have it, ladies and gents. The lady has spoken." He picked up his tote bag with one hand and wrapped the other arm around Chloe's shoulders again. "I call shot-gun."

The trio passed an enjoyable evening, eating some excellent Italian cuisine and laughing over silly jokes. For the moment at least, they had almost forgotten about the threat of the unseen entity. They left the restaurant happy and stuffed.

When they returned to Chloe's apartment, they collapsed onto the sofa together to pass the time watching TV. Chloe was terribly jittery and she found that she couldn't keep her hands still no matter how she tried. She kept twirling her hair and fussing with her shirt, every now and again pausing to sigh heavily and wiggle her foot. Jason and Trina watched all this, worried that she might be moving into the next phase of occupation even sooner than they had expected.

At midnight, Chloe announced her intentions to retire and then disappeared into her room. Jason waited until she was safely behind the closed door, then he turned to Trina to share his thoughts.

"I think one of us should keep watch on Chloe tonight. Her room has no outside walls, so the only way out of here is through the living room. I'll take the first shift."

"No, Jason. You've got jet-lag. I'll take the first shift. You take the second."

"Aw, Trina. Always looking out for me, aren't you?"

"Not at all. There's a movie coming on at one that I want to see. I'll wake you at four."

Jason trudged into the guest room, his feet leaden and his head nearly so. He fell asleep almost instantly, though he awakened frequently throughout the next two hours, remembering fragments of some wispy dream.

The credits were just rolling when Trina thought she heard a noise coming from the hallway. "Jason?" she called out softly, waiting silently for a response.

When none came, she decided to investigate. She was in a half-standing position when Chloe showed herself in the doorway of the living room. Her eyes were unblinking, though she swayed ever so slightly as she stood still.

"Oh, Chloe. I thought you were Jason. The TV wasn't keeping you up, was it?" Trina took two steps away from the chair, then froze in her tracks.

Chloe continued across the living room, still not blinking, not responding to Trina in any way.

Trina placed a staying hand on her arm. "Chloe, are you all right?"

She shrugged Trina off and continued in the direction of the front door, her face stony and her eyes misty.

"Chloe. Where are you going?" No response. Trina stepped

around her and positioned herself between Chloe and the door. "I'm not letting you leave here."

At last, Chloe's blank eyes came into focus, locking onto Trina with an intensity so sudden, so fierce that it curdled her blood. In one chillingly fast movement, she seized hold of Trina's throat and hoisted her several feet off the floor, only to pin her against the wall.

"Jason!" she shrieked, trying to call for help before her air left her. "Help!"

Chloe paid no heed to the sound of Jason's fast-approaching footsteps. She kept Trina pinned to the wall for a moment longer, then, in one easy wave of her arm, cast her aside like some stuffed animal. She landed in a dazed heap on the other side of the room, her vision flashing in and out like a strobe light.

Jason grabbed Chloe's arm forcibly and spun her about. Without warning or hesitation, he slapped her hard across the face, intending only to snap her out of her trance.

Instead of the desired effect, Chloe merely crumpled onto the floor, unconscious. At once, Jason bent down beside her on the floor, taking her pulse and feeling inexplicably guilty.

"It's okay. She's just..."

Chloe's arm shot out and latched onto Jason's throat, tossing him to the floor where she could roll atop him. They struggled violently, rolling about the room while each of them jockeyed for position. She was unbelievably strong, terrifyingly relentless in her quest to dispossess Jason of his oxygen. As they wrestled, Trina managed to gain control of her faculties again, shaking off the dizziness and the ringing in her ears. Panting, she went immediately to the spare room, where her gear was being temporarily billeted.

When she returned, Trina bore with her a syringe filled with Thorazine. Brandishing it, she called loudly to Jason. "Try and hold her still."

Jason used every ounce of strength he had ever had and then some to bring Chloe into position on the floor. Face red, arms bulging, he forced himself to exert as much pressure as was humanly possibly on her arm, thus pinning it to the floor.

More than anything else, Chloe now resembled a cornered beast. Jason recognized that look in her eyes from before, in the hospital when he had first met her. She thrashed and rolled, her head whipping from side to side and her black eyes bulging. Jason expected her to begin frothing at the mouth any second, but he held fast, refusing to let her go.

Trina plunged the needle into her arm and injected the syringe's full load. Almost at once, Chloe began to relax, her body losing strength and her arms becoming ever more manageable. It wasn't until she had fully lost consciousness, however, that Jason felt safe in releasing her.

He sat back on his haunches and wiped at his forehead with one quaking arm. When his eyes met Trina's, he felt a shared terror in them. "You okay, Trina?"

"I think so. How about you?"

"I'll live. I think I better start spending a little more time at the gym, though."

"It's like she had no control over herself. You could look in her eyes and just tell that Chloe wasn't in there." Trina felt like crying then.

"The lights are on but nobody's home. How long will she be out of it?"

"Ordinarily, I'd say about six hours. But considering her present condition, I'd say she could come out of it any time."

"I don't think we have a choice. We're going to have to restrain her."

"It's going to scare the hell out of her, waking up and finding herself tied to the bed."

"What else are we going to do? We can't just let her run amok. And it's for sure we can't stop her."

"All right. Help me get her to bed. We'll cuff her to the brass headboard."

Jason scooped the limp Chloe into his arms, his over-exerted muscles crying out in protest. He managed to get her onto the bed before his legs gave out and then stood by while Trina cuffed the girl's left wrist to one of the metal bars on the headboard. He had no idea if her present strength would allow her to simply snap the cuffs in two, but he hoped that they would hold. If they didn't, he couldn't imagine what else would contain her.

"So, you just carry a couple of pairs of cuffs around with you?" Jason laughed as he watched Trina cuff the girl.

Trina stood upright, hands on her hips, face pressed into service as an instrument of torture. "It's a long story but...yeah."

Chapter Six

Exhausted, Jason and Trina sank back into the cushions of the sofa. Chloe was still resting peacefully in her bed; was still shackled to the headboard. Jason stared at the ceiling and tried to remember a time when he had felt this tired.

"I don't think we have any recourse now, Trina. We're going to have to move Chloe to that facility you were talking about."

"I agree. They've got a completely secured isolation ward there. Even if we can't help her, we can at least keep her from hurting herself."

"Or anyone else."

"I don't think anything we've done so far has done her any good. If I had to venture a guess, I'd say we're out of options."

"Maybe Professor Stillman can tell us more. Let's count on speaking to him first thing in the morning. We'll leave right after we've spoken to him."

Trina nodded thoughtfully, her lower lip clenched between her teeth. "If it's all right with you, I'd like to catch a little cat nap."

"Sure. You go lie down for a while. Believe me, I'll call you if anything happens."

Jason was startled from his sleep by Chloe's calls from the bedroom. He was shocked to see that the sun had already risen. Even more so that he had actually fallen asleep. He pulled himself painfully from the couch, the first screams of his strained muscles giving him pause.

"I'm coming, Chloe." He reached the door to her bedroom

and peered cautiously in, not knowing what to expect.

"Was I a bad girl last night, Jason?" She was cheerful, almost bubbly.

"I'm afraid so. Hang on a sec and I'll get you out of those cuffs." He fished through his pocket until he touched on the key, then he unlocked the cuffs. "There you go. Sorry we had to do that."

"It's all right," she said, rubbing her wrists. The skin was red and marked with the impression of the cuffs. "I understand. But would you like to fill me in on what went on around here last night?"

"Over coffee. Okay?"

"I'll make it."

She sauntered into the kitchen, seemingly unaffected by the fact that she had awakened chained to her bed. Trina was just exiting her room, dressed in a white robe, her feet bare.

"Good morning, Trina," Chloe chirped as she passed her in the hall.

"She's awfully perky." Trina frowned, watching Chloe as she moved through the house.

"She doesn't remember a thing."

Chloe turned around from her doings at the coffee maker and gifted them with a large smile. "So, how bad was I?"

"Very bad," Trina offered, sliding onto one of the stools and stifling a yawn. "You tried to leave again."

"I did? Where was I going?"

"You didn't take time out to give us your itinerary," Jason slurred jokingly.

"You came out of your room and just walked toward the door. But I don't think you knew at all what you were doing. I made the mistake of trying to stop you and you...well...let's just say you roughed us both up pretty good."

Chloe's smile faulted just then, her heart sinking and her head beginning to throb. "Oh my God! How bad did I hurt you?"

Trina pulled back her robe a bit to uncover one shapely leg. There was a huge purple bruise there and the mere sight of it made Chloe wince.

"I'm so sorry. God, I wish this would just end. I can't take much more. Just knowing that I hurt someone and that this... this...thing is making me do all this...I just want to..."

Behind her, the kitchen window shattered outward, scattering glass across much of the building's side yard. Chloe looked at it ruefully, her whole face seeming to tremble at once. She slumped over the kitchen sink, all her muscles beginning to seize up with the stress that was working its way through her fragile mind and body.

Jason walked over to where she stood and put one reassuring hand on her shoulder. "Chloe, we've decided to take you out of here. We're going to move you to a facility in Tampa. Trina has friends who can give us a secure isolation chamber there. You'll be safer there."

She raised her head and craned her neck as far as she could until her sullen eyes came round to meet his. "What you mean is, the world will be safer with me in there."

Jason shot a guilty glance over at Trina. "That, too. But we'll also be able to offer you more options there."

"I'm concerned," Trina sighed. "I can usually read anybody. But I can't read you. I don't get any thoughts coming from you. Just this dull roar…like loud surf or a weak radio station that has static."

"What can we do? Is there anything left to try?" Her face looked so worried, so drawn and thin.

"We don't really know what we're dealing with here," Jason began. "But there are a lot of conventional things we could try. For all we know, simple cold will get rid of it. Or maybe electricity."

"And I have a few spells we could use. Maybe even an exorcism. But Jason is right. Since we don't know what we're dealing with, conventional methods might be best for the moment. We might also try a decompression chamber. So, you see, all hope isn't lost. You can't give up. We still have a lot of things we can try to get rid of this thing."

She sighed deeply, her lungs aching with the effort. "Thank you, Trina. But hope is really all I've ever had. And the only thing really worth dying for is life."

She tried to smile for them, to feel comforted by their news, but it simply wasn't in her. She stood straight up, her eyes refusing to leave the shattered window pane.

"If it's all right with you, I don't think I feel much like fixing breakfast this morning. But there's some frozen waffles and microwave sausage in the Frigidaire."

"It's okay, Chloe. We'll manage just fine." Jason watched her walk to the couch, most of the life and all of the strength now gone from her. What had once been a happy, energetic young woman was now just a dark, tragic soul. "Why don't you fetch the waffles, Trina. I'll give Professor Stillman a ring."

She stepped around the counter, armed with a snappy rebuttal to his chauvinist diatribe, but then thought better of it. In the end, she relented and pulled a large package of waffles from the freezer.

Jason, on the other hand, had already picked up the phone, so any rebuke on her part would have been lost on him. He hastily dialed the professor's number from the card which Mrs. Warren had given him, then watched Chloe's face as the phone rang.

"Yes? What can I do for you?"

"Is this Professor Donald Stillman?"

"Yes. Who's this?"

"My name is Jason Callahan. I'm a private investigator from New York City." He leaned casually against the wall and crossed his legs at the ankle.

"Yes?" The man seemed unimpressed by that little bit of information.

"I'm calling in regard to the death of Dr. Reed Warren. I was told that you could give me some information about that."

"You've obviously been speaking to Mrs. Warren. She never takes my calls and she's frightfully bad about keeping appointments. Give me a moment to pick this up in my den."

"Certainly." Jason waited, hearing endless silence as the man took his time getting to the den.

"Mr. Callahan? You there?"

"Yes."

"All right. Since you're calling me, I take it that you have another victim with you."

"Victim?"

"Yes, yes. Of this creature. This thing, whatever it is."

"You know about it?"

"Know about it? It killed my wife."

"You know what it is? Where it came from?"

"I'm not exactly sure about what it is. I do know where it came from, though."

"You have my undivided attention." He slid onto one of the stools in anticipation of a long conversation.

"About a year ago, I was involved in a lengthy dig in Malaysia. My wife went with me as usual, but this time we also took our nineteen-year-old son with us. We had been there about a month when we finally broke through one of the walls of the tomb. Inside, we found the body of a young man. We were later able to date the body to roughly the fifteenth century. From all appearances, he was entombed there, chained to the wall and left there to die.

"The thing is, when we entered that tomb...my son and I... there was a great rushing of air. That's not uncommon with a place that has been sealed up for so long. But with the air came a rush of what looked like black smoke. I thought it curious but I really didn't give it much thought until a week after that, when my son became ill. He took to his bed complaining of chest pains and headaches. He was running quite a high fever, so I took him to the local hospital. They weren't able to find anything wrong with him but, since he was still so ill, I called a halt to the dig and took my family home at once.

"The doctors here...and Dr. Warren was one of them... discovered a sizable tumor in my Bryan's head. Specialists were called in at once and they began surgery to remove it. During the operation, though, Bryan leaped from the operating table, his cranium still exposed, and ran from the room. Bear in mind that he was under heavy anesthesia.

"They were finally able to bring him down, though not without a great deal of struggle and medication. They continued the surgery and did remove the tumor, which they still have not identified. The best guess they could offer was that it was some sort of extraneous gland or other, though they couldn't quite say what its purpose might be. We took Bryan home and he seemed to recover quite a bit, though he was still exhibiting mild aberrant behavior."

"What sort of aberrant behavior?"

"Well, things in his room would just sort of explode. Fires would break out for no reason and he would get up in the middle of the night and simply leave the house. All without his knowledge. The only conclusion I could reach was that, whatever had happened to my son, had happened in Malaysia. So, I left at once for the dig site. I went back into the tomb and that's when I turned up some startling evidence. There were pictographs on all the walls, most of which my assistants had not yet deciphered. There was also a very odd stretch of charred sand, leading from where the corpse had been to where Bryan and I had been standing. I took a sample of this glass-like substance and had it subjected to every test I could think of. All I turned up was some odd sort of thread running through the glass, rather like lint or debris of some kind. Although it couldn't quite be described as organic, it couldn't exactly be termed manufactured either.

"When I finally managed to decipher the pictographs, they told the story of a young man who had been possessed of an evil spirit. During his possession, the man apparently attacked and killed a large portion of the village's population. In order to avoid any more such attacks, the men of the village captured him and entombed him in the king's crypt, where he had been ever since. The only conclusion I could draw was that that self-same spirit had somehow managed to survive and had entered my son's body when we broke open the tomb.

"When I returned home, Bryan's condition had worsened considerably. He was thin and anxious all the time. He was running an incredibly high fever and seemed to be throwing up a lot. Though we took him to the hospital, there was little that they could do for him. They did give him another CAT scan, though, which showed that his tumor had returned. The doctors all agreed that another operation would be risky at best, so they could offer little in the way of hope for us.

"With no other options left to us, we simply took Bryan

home. A day later, while he and my wife were sitting alone together in the living room, the thing simply left him. It exited my son's body and went directly into my wife's. Both of them saw it happen, though I was out of the room at the time."

"What were they doing when it happened?"

"Just sitting on the couch, watching TV. For no apparent reason the thing just changed hosts. So far as I know, Bryan is the only person ever to have survived its possession. Within hours, his condition had improved immeasurably. In a week, it was as if nothing at all had happened. My wife, however, did not survive. She died some two months after she became inhabited. Mr. Callahan, I've tracked this thing all across the country. Every single person whose body it has entered has died of exactly the same causes. I hate to be the harbinger of doom, but I'd say that your subject only has about another month to go."

"She began exhibiting the psychic episodes almost from the start."

"Then she may have even less time. Mr. Callahan, this thing has to be stopped. There's no telling how many more people it can kill. It's already survived for hundreds of years without a host. Who knows how long it had been around before that. You've got to get rid of it. You've got to put it in a place where it won't escape, where it can't hurt anyone else. Your life is at risk, Mr. Callahan. So is the life of anyone who comes into contact with this girl. There's only one way out. You've got to lock her away. Secure the chamber by all means possible to ensure that it will never again escape."

"I find that hard to swallow. There must be some way of killing this thing."

"Don't make that mistake, Callahan. You're gambling with your own life here. Whoever this girl is, whatever she is to you, you can't let that sway you. This creature is deadly. And it has to be stopped. If you don't have the schmaltz to do it, I'll do it for you."

"Surely, you can't mean to simply condemn her to certain death without at least trying to help her first? That would be murder." For a moment, he had forgotten that Chloe was still nearby and as the words left his mouth, he at once wished that he could take them back.

"Murder, yes. As dropping the atomic bomb on Hiroshima was murder. But it also saved the lives of millions of people. As we would be doing if we locked this girl away."

"I won't accept that. There must be some way of stopping this thing that won't also kill the girl. If the entity left your son and went into your wife, then there must be a way to duplicate those conditions. If it happened once, it can happen again."

The doctor was quite agitated now, nearly yelling into the phone. "Don't be a fool, Callahan! You have no time! Do what is right. Do what you know must be done. Before it's too late..."

Jason hung up on Professor Stillman, infuriated at the man's attitude. He just couldn't accept that Chloe would have to die in order to assure the safety of the general population. There were a great many things which he could stretch his imagination to accept. This was not one of them.

"I take it that you and Professor Stillman don't share the same views," Trina offered quietly, her face scowling into his.

"Let's just say that Professor Stillman is driven more by guilt and revenge than by logic. I say we move Chloe to Tampa right away. We'll try everything we can think of to get rid of this thing. I mean, something made this thing leave Bryan Stillman's body while he was still alive. If we can find that thing, then we can make it leave Chloe, too."

Trina lowered her voice to a near whisper. "At what price? Where will it go next? Do we just keep moving it from one person to the next until we find something to destroy it? Or until we run out of people to house it? Maybe Stillman wasn't too far off base. Maybe we don't have any other choice."

"I think you're wrong, Trina. You're both wrong." He rose from the stool and walked silently to where Chloe was seated on the sofa, trying to pretend that she couldn't hear what they were saying. He dropped onto the cushion next to her and cocked his head in her direction.

"As soon as you get your things together, I think we should leave."

"Whatever you say, Jason." She blinked rapidly at him, offered up a demure little smile.

"I hate to do this to you, but we're going to have to sedate you and restrain you during the trip. If this thing takes control of you again, there's no telling what could happen."

"It's all right. You don't have to blame yourself for any of this. You're only doing what has to be done. And you're the only person who's on my side in this." She cast a disdainful look in Trina's direction, sending cold chills up her back.

"Why don't you go pack, then. Would you like some breakfast before we leave?"

"I don't have much of an appetite, I'm afraid." She rose stiffly from the sofa and padded into her room, where her suitcases were already lying on the bed, fully packed. She couldn't recall having gotten them from the back of her walk-in closet, nor could she recollect having packed them. There they were, nonetheless, awaiting further instructions.

Chloe caught Jason's eyes with her own as he snapped the handcuff shut around the door handle. He felt horribly guilty about having to do it, but they both knew that it was the best thing.

Trina had already given the girl her medication and she was, by now, nearly under. In another few minutes, she would be deeply asleep and would probably not awaken until long after they arrived at Tampa General.

"I think we're all ready now," Trina sighed, casting one last glance back toward the apartment building. "I called your super and let him know about the window. He said he'd get it replaced right away. And Professor Arnst has the facility all ready and waiting for us. It's in the basement of a research hospital in Tampa. He said we can have it as long as we need it."

Chloe looked dreamily up at her and grinned complacently. "George is a real nice man. As long as I've lived here, he's always taken care of things right quick." She leaned precariously against the back of the car seat as her grin and her strength failed.

"Ladies? Shall we?" Jason waved toward the front seat,

indicating to Trina that she had stalled long enough.

They pulled away from the apartment, Chloe feeling something akin to separation anxiety and Jason and Trina suffering from nothing less than near hysterical anxiety. Neither of them knew how long the sedative would keep Chloe unconscious; neither of them knew if the other treatments would work. They only knew that they had to try.

"We've made everything ready, just as you said, Trina." Professor Arnst clasped his hands in front of him and stood very properly erect. "I know you said that you wouldn't be needing any assistance, but several of us can be here at a moment's notice if you need us."

"I appreciate that, Harry. I also appreciate your discretion in this."

"Not at all. If you need anything further, please do not hesitate to call." He bowed slightly and then marched off toward the elevator.

Chloe was sitting in a nearby wheelchair. She was still groggy and for the most part unfocused, but she had a cursory understanding of what was happening. Jason knelt down in front of her, offering a reassuring smile.

"Ready to see your temporary new home, Chloe?"

"By all means. Drive on."

The isolation room was in a section of the basement. It dated back to the early days when a small amount of research was conducted there and to when some diseases which now have cures were mysterious and fatal illnesses. Most of the research which had gone on there had been secret; not of the variety that the general population would be comfortable knowing about.

Jason pushed the wheelchair into the elevator, Trina walking quietly beside him. She was clutching her bag just a little too tightly, so Jason placed one gentle hand on her arm.

"Ease up, Trina. It's not the gas chamber."

She smiled meekly and stared straight ahead.

When the elevator doors slid open, they set eyes on what the employees liked to call, "The Dungeon". It was dark, lit only by weak hanging fixtures which directed them down a long corridor. The corridor climaxed in a large room, the smaller portion of which was a plexi-glass enclosure. It was secured by an electronic locking mechanism and was, they were told, totally impenetrable. They were betting their lives on that last.

"See? Not so bad," Jason chirped, trying to sound upbeat but failing miserably.

"Well, at least there's a TV. That'll make it bearable."

Inside the room, there was nothing more than the aforementioned TV and a very institutional-looking bed. Scattered about the outside room were various monitors and the like, all of which seemed totally ominous in the gothic setting of the basement ward.

"Let's get you settled in. I want to start your treatments right away." Trina helped Chloe out of the chair, then to the bed.

"I'm feeling a lot steadier now. I think I can dress myself."

Trina looked at her, gauging her truthfulness in this, and finally conceded. "All right. Call me when you're done."

She strode out of the room to where Jason was waiting for her on the outside. He had politely turned his back so that he would run no risk of catching sight of Chloe through the two-way mirror.

"Our accommodations don't look much better than hers." He was referring to the two bunks which stood on either side of the outer door. To their left was a spartan bathroom and to the right a small refrigerator. "Who worked down here anyway? Victor Frankenstein?"

"Jason, you've got to remember that this place hasn't been used in years. I find it nothing short of amazing that they were able to make it even this appealing on such short notice."

"The Ritz it ain't."

"Yoo-hoo! Trina! I'm ready." Chloe's voice came to them compliments of the intercom, startling them both.

"All right, Chloe. I've got a few more things to get done. Then, we'll begin your treatments."

"Trina, is this going to work?" Jason whispered.

"I don't know, Jason. I just don't know. Technically, an exorcism is supposed to be performed by a priest. I'm no priest.

I've done them before and it's always worked but what we're dealing with here is far different than anything I've witnessed before."

"Well, this is a first for me. I assume you have somebody to help you with this? I won't be much help."

"Of course." She sighed and looked back at Chloe, her heart breaking. "Jason, I'm pretty sure that this thing targeted Chloe from the start. It chose its victims carefully, heading east. It's like it sensed she was out here, that she was the one person who could provide it with a permanent home."

"Because of her dying and coming back all those times?"

"Precisely. She isn't suffering the same symptoms that the others did. She has no fever, no chest pains. I think her body has accepted it. And if it can get her mind to accept it, we may not get Chloe back at all."

"Then, we shouldn't hesitate. We should get started right away."

"Yes, we should."

"How did you ever get permission to use this place, anyway?"

She smiled and tossed back her hair. "Professor Arnst is a member of…let's call it a secret society, for lack of a better term. I've worked with him before. He's also a brilliant research scientist and the hospital lets him use the meager facilities down here from time to time. He was kind enough to give me carte blanche use of his drugs and equipment."

Everything that Trina had requested was already there. She fussed and fumed over them, double-checking all the equipment before she rolled it into Chloe's room. The girl watched her with a kind of morbid fascination, not really afraid, just apprehensive.

"Okay now, Chloe. I'm going to start you on an IV. That way, we can be sure that you don't get dehydrated or malnourished. Professor Arnst has prescribed this little cocktail for you. He thinks it might at least weaken the thing enough that we can drive it out. Best case scenario, it will kill it. But that's almost more than we can hope for right now. As things progress, we'll increase the frequency and dosage. Okay?" She checked

Chloe's eyes; found them compellingly warm.

"How will we know if it's working?"

"I'm not really sure. But I'd say that if nothing untoward happens in the next few hours, we'll have to move on to another therapy."

"I'm going to lose my hair and get sick like cancer patients do. Aren't I?"

"Possibly. You've got to remember that we don't know anything at all about how this entity interacts with your system. You might not suffer any ill effects at all."

"Whatever. If I can get rid of this thing, it'll all be worth it."

"Now, whenever either of us is in the room with you, we'll be wearing one of those decontamination suits like the one on the wall over there. It's just so that the creature won't be able to enter either of us if it happens to leave you while we're still here."

"I understand. But what are you going to do with it once it leaves me? How can you get me out without letting it out?"

Trina suddenly became rigid, tense. She hadn't thought of that one simple fact because she wasn't at all certain that the entity ever would leave Chloe. In fact, if she had to admit it, she would say that Chloe was probably going to die like the others. Professor Stillman was right. The only way to get rid of the thing was to entomb it – and Chloe – as soon as possible and for all time.

"I don't think it's gonna work either, Trina."

Trina's eyes snapped to Chloe's as she realized what had just happened. "I'm so sorry, Chloe. I forgot that you could hear..."

"It's okay. A person's entitled to their own private thoughts. It's just that I can't shut it out. I hear the thoughts of every person within a hundred yards. Nothing I do will make it shut up. But I do think you're right. This doesn't have a snowball's chance in hell of working. But we've got to try, right? We can't just give up?

"That's right, Chloe. Now, if you'll give me a minute to get suited up, I'll get your IV started."

Chloe smiled and nodded, watching Trina turn to leave. Beyond her, she could see Jason's worried face staring in at her. She knew she wasn't supposed to be able to see it; that the mirror was meant to obscure her view. But she could see him just as plainly as she could hear his thoughts: *Poor Chloe.*

Trina returned presently, safely enveloped in her protective suit and bearing other menacing-looking medical equipment. Chloe had been in the hospital on only two occasions other than her recent brush with death, so she had only a cursory knowledge of such things. She decided not to ask too many questions, however, since she was sure that she didn't want to know what all these things were for.

"This is just a nice IV drip. It gives me a constant means of getting the medication into your system without forcing me to have to inject you every time."

She inserted the needle skillfully into Chloe's arm as the girl stared wistfully at the ceiling. She wasn't squeamish when it came to needles and the like, except when they were being inserted into her own flesh. That made her head swim and her stomach roil.

Trina finished taping the IV tube to Chloe's arm, then readied the medications. One last check of her face told her that the girl was somewhere else, detached from her body and from what was being done to her. If that gave her some solace, then Trina was not about to interfere.

"And that's all there is to it." Trina stood back and beamed at her, happy that the deed was done.

"That's wasn't so bad. Hardly felt a thing." Okay, so it was a lie, but she needed Trina to know that she wasn't suffering at all.

"I've heard that peppermint will help calm your stomach after the treatments." She reached into the deep pocket of her decontamination suit and pulled out a plastic baggy full of mints. "So, I brought these for you."

Chloe turned on her thousand-watt smile, touched that Trina had taken the time and effort to do such a kind thing. "Thank you, Trina." She took the bag and opened it, breathing in the strong scent of peppermint.

"I think you should try and get some rest now. The TV remote is right there if you need it. And there's an intercom built into the bed if you need anything else."

"I'll be fine, Trina. Really. Don't you worry about me. My mama always said I was strong enough to take a whoopin' and then kill the guy by spitting out my teeth at him."

Trina laughed heartily and genuinely. "Your mama must have been quite a woman."

Chloe nodded, popping one of the mints into her mouth for good measure. Then, she tossed a wink in Jason's direction, catching him off-guard and making him back up a step.

Trina left the room and secured the door, leaning against it exhaustedly. She removed the hood from her suit and set it on the bed. "Well, that's one down. Six to go. Wanna play some cards?"

"How can you be so blasé about this, Trina?"

"Simple. I have to."

"And where in the hell did you learn how to start an IV?"

"Well, when you're doing an exorcism or any other type of expulsion, you're typically dealing with a person in a weakened condition. Having an IV is essential. Professor Arnst taught me. Right after high school, I went to work for him. I started out as a lab assistant but for a while, I was his partner."

"You never stop amazing me, Trina." He smiled that very confident, comforting smile of his. "So, shall we play some cards?"

"Why not?"

They sat opposite each other on Jason 's bunk and played rummy for a couple of hours. Every now and again, they would pause in their battle to take a protective glance at Chloe. She was watching TV calmly, but she couldn't hear the dialogue. The voices in her head drowned them out.

Chapter Seven

Jason and Trina were both asleep when Chloe called out to them. She had used the intercom and was very nearly screaming to make herself heard above the noises in her head. Her face was as white as snow and her eyes hollow and sunken.

"Trina! Jason! Please help me."

Trina ran to the intercom and jammed the button down. "What's wrong, Chloe?"

"The voices," she sobbed, grabbing onto her head with both arms and squeezing her eyes tightly shut. "I can't make them stop."

"You mean, you're hearing other people's thoughts?"

"No. Not those voices. The other ones. I can hear the thing that's in me. It's talking to me. Trying to tell me something. But I can't make it out. And I hear other voices. The voices of the people it's killed. They all keep yelling for me to save them, to set them free. Oh, God! Please make them stop. Just make them stop." She slid, wailing and crying, down the wall into a tortured little heap.

Trina and Jason shared a terrified glance, then Trina jumped into her decon suit. She prepared a sedative before going in, knowing that this was the only way to silence the voices in Chloe's head.

"Be careful, Trina. It might be a trick."

She shot a glance at Jason, startled by that revelation. "Don't worry. I will."

She entered the room and went to Chloe, placing her arms around the girl and struggling to help her to her feet. She managed to get her onto the side of the bed, and then swing her legs up onto it. Poor Chloe was rigid from the fear and anguish, though her mouth worked feverishly, trying to sound out what the voices were saying to her.

"Can't understand it. It doesn't speak English and it mumbles. It's more like a whisper but it's all deafening inside my head." She was shouting, the sound of her own voice drowned out by the din in her head.

"It's okay, Chloe. I'm going to give you something to help you sleep." She flushed the IV tube with a syringe full of saline, then injected the sedative into it. "There. You'll be feeling better in a few minutes."

She sat down on the bed, stroking her hair and watching Chloe's twisted face as she fought to gain control over the haunting voices. As she finally began to calm down and actually focus on Trina, her facial muscles relaxed a bit, giving her face a more human, less monstrous appearance.

"Oh, God! This is awful. The worst part ever."

"Is the sedative helping?"

"Yeah. I think. The voices are getting quieter." She was still speaking too loudly, as though she couldn't hear her own voice.

"Can you tell me anything that they said?"

"Not the entity. But the people. The souls of the people it killed are here. He stole them, Trina. And now, they're inside me. And they can't get free to go to heaven. I wanna help them, but I just don't know how." She was beginning to feel groggy. She yawned.

"Did they say anything in particular? Can you ask them questions?"

"I don't know. I was too busy trying to make them shut up."

"If it happens again, try to talk to the voice of Mrs. Stillman. Try to find out how her son Bryan was able to get the entity out of him without dying."

Chloe nodded weakly, her eyes blinking even more slowly. "I'll do my best. Can't make...any...promises."

Trina stayed at her side a moment longer, then she went out to rejoin Jason.

"How is she?" Jason was sitting on the edge of his bunk, his face covered with stubble and his eyes severely bagged.

"I'm just not sure. Maybe the new therapy brought all this on. Maybe not. She says the entity was trying to tell her something but she couldn't hear or couldn't understand its language. But she says that she could hear the voices of all the people the thing has killed. They were asking for her help to get free of that thing."

"Can you imagine how terrible a thing that must be? I mean, she's got all those other people in there with her. It's almost like multiple personality disorder, only these people are all real."

"Well, if nothing else, this has told me what this thing is. It's a reaper, Jason. And I was right. It intentionally targeted Chloe."

"A reaper? As in…?"

"Souls. It collects souls. And it's been doing it for thousands of years. I told her to try and talk to them if it happens again. Maybe Mrs. Stillman can tell her what it was that Bryan did to save himself."

"And maybe the Beatles will reunite."

She looked at Jason, her face locked tight in a grimace of displeasure, but her eyes sparkling with laughter.

Chloe was sedated most of the next day and spent the rest of the day throwing up. The peppermints helped to some degree, but a person could only eat so many peppermints. A call to Professor Arnst provided no definitive answers; none of them could be sure whether it was the medicine or the entity which was making her sick. Trina and Jason took turns ministering to her, comforting her. They could watch her, hour by hour, as she grew weaker and more intangible. The voices returned briefly to haunt her, though she found that the sounds of those who had gone before her had become more of a comfort to her than the creature was a bother. The communication seemed to be one-way, however, since all her attempts to engage them in a dialogue failed miserably.

There was also the fact that her psychic powers seemed to be increasing exponentially. On several occasions, Trina or Jason would enter the room, only to find strange objects in her bed which had not been there before. She conjured them out of thin air, seemingly without conscious effort or awareness. They were mostly harmless things, such as books or food. But the frequency of their appearance was increasing, as was her discomfort and misery from the treatments.

They all turned in that night feeling badly beaten and worn. Sleep found Trina and Jason virtually the instant they pulled the crisp, white sheets around their ears. Chloe, however, was not that fortunate.

She remained awake, watching late shows and occasionally vomiting. Her arm hurt where the IV had infiltrated earlier, forcing Trina to move it to a location on the other wrist. Her head ached violently and she was given to fits of blindness from the severity of their pain. Through it all, though, she kept listening to Trina and Jason's thoughts and, less consciously to the message from her possessor.

At four in the morning, Chloe rose from her bed, under her own power and as determined as she had ever been. She walked to the mirror and stared through it for several minutes, watching Trina and Jason as they dreamed. Then, she walked to the door and placed her thin, pale hands upon it. She followed this by resting her face against it, an expression of near rapture taking hold of her features.

Within moments, several sparks flew from the keypad on the other side of the door, locking the door and disabling the coding mechanism. A smile of pure satisfaction flitted across her small face as she walked back to her bed and slowly, carefully, laid herself out upon it.

She craned her neck, looking up and backward at the IV bag which hung from its metal hook. Her eyes traveled the length of the tube until they reached the exact point where the needle penetrated her flesh. She knew what she was doing. There was no one and nothing exerting any control over her, it more than likely would have tried to stop her.

She knew this to be fact and that was why she exercised such diligence in keeping her mind a total blank. That was also why she had to act with such swiftness, to prevent the thing from foiling her plan.

In one strong, fast jerk, she pulled the IV tube from its bag spraying a tiny amount of the fluid across the bed sheet as it was torn free. She watched in complete fascination as the saline solution began to trickle out of the tube, forced out by the pressure of her own blood. She knew that, once the pressure from the IV drip had been stopped, the pressure of her heart would back-wash her blood out of her body through the tube.

She lay perfectly still, grasping the severed end of the plastic tube in one hand and watching, entranced as the blood poured from it. It was a perfect plan. No one would be able to get that door open in time to save her. By the time the proper people arrived to fix the door, she would long since have bled to death.

She was wrong.

Trina awakened to the call of nature several minutes after Chloe had pulled her own IV. She staggered sleepily to the window to check on Chloe. Then, her eyes bulged as she saw what was going on inside that room.

Without thinking, she punched in the four digit code and waited for the door to open. When nothing happened, she tried again. And again.

The door stubbornly refused to yield, so Trina began to panic. "Jason! Get up! I can't get the door open and Chloe's pulled her IV."

Jason jettisoned himself from his bed and rocketed to the window. In one swift movement, he grabbed up the phone and dialed the number listed on the phone for maintenance.

"This is Jason Callahan down in the basement. I need someone down here right now. The door's malfunctioned and our patient has attempted suicide."

"Right away..." the voice on the other end started to say, but Jason hung up and didn't hear.

Trina was already struggling into her decon suit in anticipation of the door's opening. She pushed the intercom button savagely and then yelled into it. Her voice was high with worry and tremulous with fear.

"Chloe? Can you hear me?"

Chloe turned her hazy eyes toward the window and smiled. It was such a peaceful, vacant smile that it made Trina's blood freeze in her veins. "Please don't be mad, Trina. It's the only way. After I'm dead, you can seal this room off forever. It'll never get out to hurt anybody again."

"Chloe! You can't do this! Please, honey, you've got to listen to me. Take the IV tube and pinch it shut. That'll stop the bleeding until we can get in there."

"No, Trina. This is how it has to be. All those people. If you could hear their voices, you'd understand." Tears rolled down her cheeks and soaked the pillowcase. "Tell Dawg I'm sorry for all the trouble. And tell Professor Stillman that his wife loves him very much."

Chloe's eyes glazed over and her head lolled to one side. Trina allowed her eyes to roam to the floor, where a goodly portion of Chloe's blood had pooled around the bed. For the first time in her professional career, Trina felt like throwing up.

"Trina! Move!"

She turned just in time to see Jason pluck the metal chair from under the desk. He was wielding it with all his might as he ran at the mirror with it. Biting into his lip, he brought the heavy metal chair crashing against the mirror, fully expecting it to shatter. He was sorely disappointed.

He made several attempts at breaking the glass but to no avail. The thing was made to keep people on the inside from getting out and vice versa. He had about as much chance of shattering that mirror as he did of seeing that Beatles reunion.

Finally, he was forced to admit his defeat and he collapsed, gasping and wheezing onto his bed. The maintenance man rushed in just then, passing them both up in deference to the control panel.

"Yep. Connections are fried," he said, more to himself than to either of them. "Have to use the manual by-pass."

Trina and Jason gaped at each other, feeling stupid for not having thought of it. The tall man stepped past them to the little alcove behind the door, sliding a small panel aside to reveal a hand crank. It was old and had not been maintained in many years. He pulled at it with all his might and was finally able to budge it just an inch. Jason leant his strength to the battle and together they managed to get the door almost fully open.

Trina ran in and grabbed up Chloe's IV tube. She cast a hectic glance over her shoulder at Jason, commanding him with her eyes. "Call up to the first floor nurse's station. Tell them I need two units of O-positive. Then get in here."

Jason was not wearing his decon suit, but he made the call while he was climbing into it and only then did he venture into the isolation room. Chloe was all but dead and his mind kept returning to the fact that she had already been dead three times, each time making a more dramatic return to the living. He prayed that she would do so just one more time.

"You better get out of here," Trina yelled back to the maintenance man. "Jason, hand me that tray over there. Hurry."

Jason did as he was instructed, passing the tray to Trina and then awaiting further orders. He noticed that her face was nearly as colorless as Chloe's and that her eyes had never looked quite so wild before.

"Okay. Take hold of this tube and be careful to keep it pinched shut until I get it out of her arm." The clear plastic face of her suit had fogged from her frantic breath but he could still see her wild-scared eyes.

Jason took the tube and did as he was told, watching attentively as Trina removed the IV from Chloe's arm. This done, she tossed the whole affair into the trash can and bent to take Chloe's pulse.

"She's dead," Trina intoned, meeting Jason's gaze. "She's dead and the door's open."

A nurse ran in with the blood, handing the bags hurriedly to Trina and then beating a hasty retreat. She wasn't sure what horrible disease that girl must have to be so isolated, but she was sure she didn't want it.

As the gravity of what Trina had said sunk in, Jason paled a bit himself. Recalling the way that Chloe had remained dead nearly an hour after the thing must have entered her body, a chill gripped his spine.

"Don't worry, Jason. She's not going to stay dead."

"Trina, you're talking nonsense. She's dead and that thing..."

"Is still inside her. If it knew that she wasn't going to come back, it would already have left her in favor of a warmer body. But it didn't."

"How can we be sure?"

"Because, we'd have seen it. And because there's no burnt streak. Trust me, Jason. The second we get Chloe's veins filled with blood, she'll be good as new."

He studied her face for a while, thinking her to have finally snapped under all the pressure. "But Trina, with her heart stopped, she has no way of pumping the blood through her veins. She'll die anyway."

"No. I can't believe that. Besides, Chloe's heart was stopped for almost an hour last time. And she still came back to life, didn't she?"

"But this is really what she wanted, isn't it? She wanted to die. Otherwise, she wouldn't have gone to such great lengths. Maybe it's a sign, Trina. A sign that we should just let her be. Seal off the room and have done with it."

"No. There must be another way. She doesn't have to die. Jason, if you've never trusted me before, trust me now. We don't have time to debate this. We'll just give her the transfusion and let Chloe handle the rest."

Unmoving, he stared at her a moment longer. He wasn't yet thoroughly convinced; wasn't at all sure he ever would be. But he did trust Trina and so he let her go ahead with the transfusion.

Jason fully expected the whole thing to be an exercise in futility. He knew in his heart that they would be pronouncing Chloe dead momentarily. Although he would be sad at Chloe's death, he would also be relieved and happy that she wouldn't have to suffer any longer.

As the blood drained slowly into Chloe's waiting veins, Jason and Trina sat back and watched the whole process in silent reverence. Trina changed bags, checking for a pulse and finding none. She leaned back against the wall, finally beginning to feel the full brunt of her exhaustion.

"I told you, Trina. It's not going to work. Chloe's dead and there's nothing we can do about it. We did all we could. Now, we might as well seal the room off." Jason turned to leave, starting to unfasten his decon suit as he walked.

"No! Wait! Look!"

Jason did look and what he saw brought him closer to actually fainting than he had ever come before. Chloe was licking her lips, her neck attempting to right her head but failing miserably. It lolled there, muscles spasming and neurons firing randomly. Ultimately, she gained enough control to pry her eyes open. Trina grabbed her wrist at once, seeking and finding a most welcome pulse.

"Chloe? Can you hear me?" Jason bent over her, a crooked smile adorning his face.

"Jason? How did you..." She forced her eyes to focus on his blurry face, then frowned morosely. "Why aren't I dead?"

"Because you're not supposed to be." He leaned in and stroked back Chloe's hair, offered up a little smile to reassure her.

"I wanted to die. Why didn't you let me die?" A small, crystal-like tear trickled down her cheek, bound for the pillow.

"We wouldn't let that happen to you. You can't lose hope. Not yet."

"But when is enough enough? I've been through so much. And it hurts. Every minute of every day hurts like hell. Life just isn't worth living if you have to go through all that pain."

"What wise person was it who said, 'The only thing worth dying for is life'?"

She looked up at his comical expression and was made to smile back at him. "Oh fine! Use my own words against me."

"You've got to promise that you won't try this again. Okay? Promise."

She was held there by his intense eyes, feeling all resolve melting in the face of his conviction. "All right, ya bully! I promise."

"Good girl. Now, you just lie back and get some rest. Tomorrow's another day and I'm sure it's going to look much brighter."

She snorted her rebuke, then turned toward the wall. She wanted to beat this thing. She wanted that more than anything else in the world. Even if it meant having to take her own life. She had forgotten, though, that she was the one person on the face of the earth who just might not be afforded the luxury of death. Perhaps that was why she had been chosen in the first place. Perhaps she was the only one in the world capable of offering this thing a permanent home. That was what frightened her most of all: The fact that this might not be over in a week or a year. The fact that it might go on for ten years or a hundred. Even if she did manage to rid herself of this beast, the scant few happy years she had left in this life would not be worth the walk through hell to get to it.

Trina eased the door shut, her eyes finding Jason's and locking there as if her life depended on it. As she stared at him, one hand peeled back the top part of her decon suit; the other produced her cell phone. She dialed from memory, then pressed the phone to her ear with a sigh. It was answered on the second ring.

"We're ready," she said softly, and hung up.

Trina paced for a while, chewing her thumbnail and scowling. Jason watched her from his place on the bunk, his eyes heavily lidded and dark. Neither uttered a word, though Jason was increasingly tempted to just scream at her. Behind the glass, Chloe slept soundly, her sleep interrupted only by the occasional roll or soft moan.

Finally, there was a knock at the door and Trina jumped and squealed at the sudden sound. She was off across the room, then, hurrying for the door and flinging it open. A tall man with broad shoulders, dark clothes and even darker hair stepped into the room and Trina rushed to hug him. She placed a kiss on each of his cheeks and reached beyond him to shut the door.

"Thank you for coming, Andrew. I couldn't do it without you." She tried to smile, found it was beyond her meager energy levels.

"And what is it, exactly, that we're doing?" Jason asked. His hands were in his pockets as he ambled slowly closer to them, smiling his best playboy smile.

"Andrew, this is my partner, Jason Callahan. Jason, this is Father Andrew Rivelli."

Jason looked him over for a moment. Cheap clothes, cheap haircut, cheap shoes. But clean and bright-eyed. Only then did Jason notice that the Father was carrying a gym bag. He thrust out his hand and nodded congenially. "Pleased to meet you, Father."

Andrew grabbed Jason's hand at once, smiling brightly as he pumped it. "Call me Andrew, please."

"Andrew." Jason liked the man immediately. He lacked the pomposity that the several priests he had met seemed to possess. And he seemed somewhat humble. "You're a Catholic priest, I take it. I'm sorry if I sound stupid, but Trina didn't tell me a thing about you…or why you're here."

Andrew shot a glance at Trina and grinned. "I am a Catholic priest, yes. Retired, though I still carry all the mantles, rights and powers." He paused to set his bag on Jason's bed and to wipe his palms on the legs of his pants. "I take it that this is the girl?" he asked, nodding in the direction of the isolation room.

"Yes." Trina swallowed and moved closer to the window. "I'll warn you. She can hear everything we say…or rather… think."

"Duly noted."

Jason detected an accent in Andrew's soft voice, but he couldn't be sure of its origins.

"Jason, please be a love and go get my box out of the trunk." She watched as he nodded, headed for the door. "Thank you." She waited until the door had closed on Jason before she continued. "I've cleared a place on the desk for you to prepare. I know you have to pray and take the sacrament."

"I did both of those two things before I left the church. And I offered confession as well. Now," he continued, taking Trina's face in both his hands, "I know you do not pray. I understand. The only thing that matters is that your heart and your purpose are pure. You have done this before and I am sure you'll be fine."

Trina plumbed the depths of Andrew's eyes and recalled their first meeting. He had been trying to exorcise a demon from a young man in France; she chasing a suspected werewolf. In the end, they had turned out to be one and the same and the boy – though he had tortured them for weeks on end – had ultimately been saved.

Behind them, the door clicked open and shut. Jason stood on the second step, taking in the whole scene, not sure what to make of it. As he began to descend the stairs, Andrew let Trina go and stepped back.

"I'm afraid we're going to have to wear the decontamination suits while we're in there. With all due respect to your faith, we need a little something more to protect us in the event that we actually drive that thing out of her."

"Understood. But I need one hand free with which to make the sign of the cross on her."

"We'll tape the cuff of one sleeve off and hope that will do it." She looked toward Jason and smiled. "I want you to stay out here. You're a bit too skeptical to be in the room with us. Besides, we only have two suits."

Jason nodded. "Fine by me."

"That means you cannot enter the room at any time, for any reason." Andrew stared him down, his jaw set like stone and his eyes penetrating. "No matter what you see or hear, no matter if one of us calls you to come in, you must not enter the room. Do you understand?"

"Believe me, Father. I get it."

"Very well. I shall begin my preparations." Andrew stepped to the back of the room with his bag and began laying his things out on the desk.

Trina leaned in so close that Jason thought she might actually kiss him. No matter how he hated to admit it, it gave him a thrill. Instead, she slid into his arms. When she spoke, it was a whisper, a prayer. "If you have any sort of faith in you, please pray for us. All of us."

She withdrew from him then and his heart sank. Skin clammy, eyes stinging, he stood in the middle of the room and watched her go to her box and pull out several items. A bag in her hands, she untied it, pulled it open, and began pouring a thick line of red dust along the base of the mirror from wall to wall. When she was done, she retied the bag and placed it back in the box. Jason saw her lips move, studied her face, trying to memorize it.

She stepped to the mirror then, just to the right of the door and though Jason couldn't see everything that she was doing, he saw what she did next. She raised two fingers, now red, and began to trace a figure on the mirror. Only then did Jason realize that she had cut her palm with a knife and was drawing the figures in her own blood. It gave him a sick feeling and made his head spin for a moment. He sat down to quell the sensation, but he couldn't take his eyes from her as she worked, chanting and drawing that symbol on each side of the door, and again on the door itself. The mood down there in the basement had turned dark. The air itself seemed malevolent.

Satisfied, she stepped back with a sigh, lips still moving, hands rising as she whispered. When she finished, the symbols burst into flames, burning brightly for a few moments before they were extinguished, leaving a blackened, burned symbol where Trina's blood had been. The sudden burst of light made Jason start, though he choked back any sound that might have otherwise escaped his lips. He blinked once, slowly, and when he opened his eyes, Andrew was standing next to him.

"I take it you've done this before?" Jason asked, standing.

Andrew smiled, nodded. "Many times. Do not worry. My faith is unshakable."

"And how do you marry that with Trina's methods?"

Again Andrew gave up that beatific smile. "The same goal, different approaches. It's like making cookies. I might mix everything in one bowl, while another person mixes the dry goods in one and the liquids in another before blending them. Either way, you still get cookies."

Jason nodded, mulling this over.

"We should begin," Trina called to them, holding out one of the suits to Andrew.

Father Andrew was praying before the zipper on his suit went up. He blessed the doorway, the mirror, Trina, Jason and himself. Jason had no part in this, save for the aforementioned staying out of the room, which he fully intended to do. Together,

Trina and Andrew stepped over the line of red dust and into the room, where they closed the door securely and began their work.

From his spot on the bed, Jason could hear everything that went on in the room. He preferred not to see. If what Trina and Andrew had said was true, there was nothing he could do about it anyway.

"Hello, Chloe," Trina began with a smile. "This is Father Andrew Rivelli. He's going to perform the exorcism we talked about."

"Hello, Father." Chloe was bright-eyed and her pleasant smile belied the pain beneath.

The Father continued to pray, paying Chloe no heed.

"Now, I want you to relax and don't be scared. We'll take care of everything." Trina smiled again and rubbed Chloe's arm gently. "The symbols I placed on the mirror and the line of brick dust will stop the entity from leaving the room, so don't be scared about that."

"Okay," Chloe said with a nod. She seemed increasingly less convinced.

Jason heard the priest begin the litany of the saints. He tried to listen and pay attention but he was so tired that his head actually thrummed with the effort of holding it up. By the time that Psalm 53 had begun, Jason had already nodded off twice. He scooted lower on the bed and shut his eyes purposefully. Andrew's voice was soothing, calming. Jason slipped into the depths of his dreams.

Andrew kept his eyes on the Bible, clutched now firmly in his hand. The other wielded the sign of the cross where appropriate, holy water when necessary.

"I command you, unclean spirit, whoever you are, along with all your minions now attacking this servant of God, by the mysteries of the incarnation, passion, resurrection, and ascension of our Lord Jesus Christ, by the descent of the Holy Spirit, by the coming of our Lord for judgment, that you tell me by some sign your name, and the day and hour of your departure. I command you, moreover, to obey me to the letter, I who am a minister of God despite my unworthiness; nor shall you be emboldened to harm in any way this creature of God, or the bystanders, or any of their possessions."

Chloe remained unmoving, her eyes steady and bright. If she was in any discomfort, she gave no indication of it. And so Andrew continued reading from the Bible and next to him, Trina fingered her talisman and mouthed an incantation.

"I cast you out, unclean spirit, along with every Satanic power of the enemy, every spectre from hell, and all your fell companions; in the name of our Lord Jesus Christ. Begone and stay far from this creature of God. For it is He who commands you, He who flung you headlong from the heights of heaven into the depths of hell. It is He who commands you, He who once stilled the sea and the wind and the storm. Hearken, therefore, and tremble in fear..."

They continued like that for nearly two hours and the only sign they received from Chloe was a sneeze. She lay on the bed, watching them both, her face blank. If she were a girl possessed, they could find no proof. Ultimately, Andrew shook his head at Trina, Trina nodded, and the door was opened.

The sudden rush of the air and the sound of the door lock disengaging aroused Jason from his sleep and he spun to the edge of the bed and blinked at them. "Well?"

"No dice." Trina opened her suit and removed her gloves. "Either there's nothing there or it isn't affected by the rite."

"So, what now?" Jason looked from one to the other, his eyes questioning, frantic.

"I do not know," Andrew admitted with a shrug. "I have never run across any possessing entity that was not subject to the powers of God."

Jason held his tongue. Live and let live, he always said.

"Thank you for trying, Andrew." Trina leaned in and kissed both of his cheeks, gave his shoulders a little squeeze. "If you think of anything else that might help, please give me a ring."

"I will." He placed his items into the bag one at a time, blessing each one, then zipped the bag shut. "Please be careful. The only thing I can think of that is not subject to the will of God is a thing that is older than God. And that would be a thing that is very powerful indeed."

Trina nodded. "We'll be careful. I promise."

She watched as Andrew ascended the stairs and slipped out the door. When she turned back to Jason, her eyes had a dreamy quality to them and her cheeks were flushed.

"Any ideas?" Jason queried.

"Sleep." Trina yawned and sat down on the bed.

Chapter Eight

From where they were, secreted in the basement of the hospital, they couldn't possibly tell if the weather were sunny or gray. But as they awoke late on that Monday morning, it somehow just felt sunny inside that small, dank space. Jason climbed from his bunk first, having been lying there awake for several minutes, just enjoying the fruits of his sloth. When he went to the mirror to check on Chloe, he was astonished to see her sitting up in bed, watching the early news and eating a full breakfast.

"Chloe!" he chuckled through the intercom, his scruffy face sporting a smile. "Where'd you get the chow?"

She looked toward him and proffered the largest, warmest smile he had ever seen. "Same place I get all the other stuff. Want some?"

He thought for a moment about this, finally deciding that it was a splendid idea. "Yeah. Sure. Why not?"

The words had no sooner left his mouth than a huge tray appeared on the desk behind him, heaped with every kind of breakfast food imaginable. He breathed in the hearty aroma and grinned. "Thanks, Chloe."

"Don't mention it." She stuffed a sizable, whole sausage into her mouth and chewed greedily on it.

"I smell bacon," Trina's voice announced from her bunk.

Jason turned in her direction, still smiling and feeling fine and dandy. "You certainly do. Want some?"

She came up behind him, peering curiously over his shoulder to peruse the tray. "I sure do."

"Chloe, if you please." He waved grandiosely in her

direction, knowing that the girl was and always had been reading their minds.

An identical tray appeared from the air space around them and Trina poked at the food with her finger, half expecting it to disappear. "Silly me. I thought you were going up to the cafeteria like any normal person."

The three of them ate breakfast together, Trina and Jason seated at the desk and Chloe resting in her bed on the other side of the glass. She was separated from the rest of the world; alone. But she had her own kind of company. Thousands of people's thoughts drifted into her head from all over the hospital. Then, there were also the voices of the other people who temporarily called her body home.

"I've been listening to the voices all night. They all seem to be making a lot more sense now. Except for the thing, that is. He's still way too garbled to make any sense out of."

"It's all right, Chloe," Jason offered from behind a mouthful of eggs. "I'm sure that will come with time. Besides, the really important thing is how you feel. How do you feel, Chloe?"

"I feel just fine. I don't know what you put in that transfusion last night but it sure seemed to do the trick. I don't feel nauseous anymore and I'm not nearly as achy."

"That's good," Trina interrupted. "Because I've decided to step up your treatments. I think maybe all these new affectations have been brought on in some way by the drugs. Maybe if we increase them, we can make it uncomfortable enough to leave."

She nodded idly, still really concentrating on the voices in her head rather than in her ears.

When they had finished breakfast, Chloe made the dirty dishes go away. She was beginning to feel just a bit proud of the fact that she could do such miraculous things, though she wasn't fond of their source. She would happily have traded all her newfound skills for a quiet, unremarkable life.

Jason let Trina have the bathroom first, then went in to shave when she was done. For some reason as yet unknown to him, he was feeling unbelievably spry and wistful that morning. He was whistling when he exited the bathroom, something which he rarely, if ever, did.

"I think I'll take a short trip into town this morning. Pick up a few things. Maybe get some laundry done, if you know what I mean."

"I do," Trina chirped, wincing at the pretend smell and fanning her nose. "We'll be fine here while you're gone. Won't we, Chloe?"

"Oh, yes. Fine." Her voice had an airy, far-away quality to it. Trina equated that to her preoccupation with her internal friends.

"All right, then. To the Laundromat. By the way, is yellow a color or a white?"

Trina looked at him, afraid that he had said that in all honesty. As it happened, he had. "Jason, white is white. Everything... and I do mean everything...else is a color."

"Just checking." He shoved a pair of chinos into an olive drab duffel and slung it dramatically over his shoulder. "No wild parties while I'm gone. And if I come home and find beer bottles in the trash, you're both grounded."

Trina shot him a snide look, screwing up her face and sticking her tongue out at him playfully. She watched, still grinning, as he left the room.

Chloe was still gazing at the TV, seemingly comfortable and untroubled for what might be the first time in a week. Trina slipped casually into her decon suit and then cranked the door open. The maintenance man had promised to return that afternoon to repair the burnt out chips but until then, she had to open the door by more conventional methods.

"So, how are you really feeling?" She stared at Chloe, amazed at her ability to become so engulfed in such banal TV shows.

"I'm feeling right as rain. And yourself?"

"A little tired, but in good humor. That breakfast sure helped."

"Glad I could do my part."

Trina took her pulse, then wrapped a cuff around her arm. "It must be kind of neat, knowing that you can have anything you want the second you want it." She pressed her stethoscope to Chloe's arm and then pumped up the cuff.

"Yeah. As soon as I figure out how to make this TV get cable, I'll be in business." She offered Trina a phantom smile and then returned her eyes to the TV screen.

"Well, you don't seem any the worse for wear after your little escapade last night."

"I'm sorry I scared you so bad. Believe me, I never intended you to find me until it was too late. I honestly did think it was the only way to get myself...and you, too...out of this whole mess. Can you forgive me?"

"Of course I can. I don't know that I wouldn't try the same thing if I were in your shoes. I'm just glad we were able to get to you before it was too late."

"Yeah." She rested her head on the pillow, her face dreamy and distant.

"I'll leave you alone now. I'm going to administer your next treatment just after lunch, so you can rest until then."

"Thanks, Trina."

She watched Chloe for a moment, beginning to get the distinct feeling that everything Chloe did, everything she said, was rehearsed or forced. It was almost as if there was a faux Chloe sitting before her now, trying hard to seem like the real Chloe but landing just a few feet to the right of the target.

She left the room anyway, suddenly feeling rather spooked. There were several vitally important crossword puzzles waiting for her in the other room. There were also the day's notes to be logged.

She had been sitting at the desk, entering her notes on the laptop for quite some time. So immersed in the task was she that she had nearly forgotten Chloe's presence, and her special talents.

"Trina?" Chloe called out, startling her so bad that she nearly knocked a soda can off the desk.

"What is it, Chloe?" From her position at the desk, she was able to see through the mirror without turning her head too much.

"I'm feeling cold. Can I have another blanket, please?" The girl was shivering visibly, her teeth very nearly chattering from her chills.

"Of course, Chloe."

Trina climbed back into the decon suit for what seemed like the thousandth time that week, then pulled a heavy army-type blanket from the shelf in the supply closet. She cranked open the door just enough that she could enter, then walked over to the bed.

"Here you are, Chloe," she said, shaking the blanket out and letting it settle onto the bed. "I really shouldn't be in here while we're alone. The door only opens from the outside, so if there were any trouble..." A frightening thought suddenly collided with her brain and her face dropped an inch or two. "Chloe, why didn't you just produce a blanket the way you did the breakfast?"

No time for reaction was allowed as Chloe leaped from the bed, her IV trailing after her like it had a life of its own. She grasped Trina's throat brutally and slammed her up against the wall. As she hung there, suspended mere inches over the floor, Trina heard the unmistakable sound of the door thudding shut. She turned her eyes in its direction, pivoting her head as much as Chloe's tight grasp would allow. The door was shut now, her escape route blocked.

"Don't be scared, Trina," Chloe dead-panned, her tone turning to mockery as she said her name. "It doesn't hurt. Really it doesn't." In one swift movement, Chloe seized hold of the suit's top and peeled it back as one might peel a banana.

"Chloe, no! Please, don't do this. Let me down."

Chloe laughed. The sound got longer and louder and more maniacal as it reverberated throughout the room. Her eyes were the really frightening thing, though. They were no longer brown. Or blue. They were a deep, tarry lack and without a hint of sparkle.

Like a stereo being turned off, Chloe's laughter ceased in a heartbeat. She concentrated her dark, malevolent eyes on Trina, allowing her to slide down the wall until her feet touched the floor. Her eyes were mesmerizing, holding Trina with their steely, cruel gaze. Chloe took a deep breath, straightened, and began pulling Trina toward her.

Trina beat at Chloe's arms, kicked out with one foot. She

knew it would do no good, but she screamed anyway, then clamped her lips tightly shut. Her heart hammered against her ribcage, her head spun as she began to hyperventilate. None of it did any good. Chloe was too strong.

Just before releasing Trina's throat, Chloe locked her lips over Trina's, pressing them tightly together and holding them there. Within seconds, the deed was done and Chloe pulled back, weak and dazed. At once, the reality of what she had been led to do infringed upon her psyche and she covered her mouth with one hand, her eyes once more blue and yet still glazed over.

She focused on Trina's face for a mere second, then slumped onto the floor at her feet, apparently lifeless. And empty.

Chapter Nine

Jason was humming quietly to himself as he strutted in through the door, the bag full of now-clean clothes slung over one shoulder. A trip into the light of day had done a world of good for his spirits, his soul. He felt light-hearted and giddy, like one who has just awakened from a horrific nightmare only to find that the world was as happy a place as they had remembered.

All that came to a swift halt, however, when his eyes came to rest on the little scene behind the mirror. His feet quit obeying his commands and all forward motion ceased.

Inside the small isolation room, Trina was sitting on the floor, her face streaked from tears and her eyes puffy and red. She was holding Chloe in her arms, rocking her gently back and forth while smoothing back her hair.

Jason dropped the bag on the floor where he stood and went straight away to the crank. He forced the door open just enough to pass through, then ran to Trina's side. He came to rest on the floor next to her like a runner sliding into first.

"Trina! What happened? Is she dead?" His heart was pounding a savage rhythm in his chest, his breathing suspended pending Trina's answer.

"She said she was cold," she offered by way of explanation. "So, I brought her a blanket. I was wearing the suit. I didn't think it would hurt if I came in here for just a minute. Jason, she seemed so normal."

"Trina! What are you saying?" His eyes were frantic with fear, his heart now threatening to burst with the stress.

"She grabbed me, locked her lips on mine. And then it was

over." She turned weary, terrified eyes up to Jason. "It's in me now, Jason. It's in me."

"God, Trina! No!" He ran a quaking hand through his hair, suddenly feeling as though he would faint dead away. "Chloe? Is she..."

"She's alive. But she's been in a coma-like state since it happened."

"How long?"

"About an hour and a half now." She licked her dry lips and swallowed roughly. "Jason, you can't be in here. Nobody can be in here. Take Chloe and put her on my bunk. Then shut the door."

He studied her eyes, knowing that she was right but lacking the fundamental courage to follow her orders. "Trina, I..."

"Just do it. No hearts and flowers now, Jason."

Without another word, he scooped Chloe into his arms and struggled to his feet. Once he had placed her on the bunk, he went to the crank and, casting one mournful look at Trina, shut the door on her. He went to the window then, pressing his hands longingly against its cold surface and leaning his scalding forehead against the glass.

"How do you feel?"

"Tired. And scared. Mostly scared."

"What do I do?"

"I'm not sure, Jason. We're basically back where we started. The thing to figure out is why it left Chloe in the first place. She wasn't exhibiting any of the symptoms that the others did on the day they died. So, why now?"

"Because it's smart," said the tiny, weak voice on the bunk. Jason turned to catch Chloe's face, which looked old beyond its years.

"Chloe? How do you feel?"

"Relieved. I'm sorry, Trina. I'm so sorry. I couldn't stop it. It's just too strong."

"I know, Chloe. I don't blame you. I blame myself."

"Chloe," Jason began, his hands working in his pockets, "you said it was smart. What did you mean?"

"I mean it knew that it couldn't stay in me. Even if it was

able to survive all our therapies, it would never be able to leave that room. And it knew that Trina had more power. More knowledge. It takes all the knowledge from the people it possesses. That's why it took Dr. Warren. It learned a lot from him about the human body and how to best use it, occupy it. It's very cunning, Jason. And it's got a plan."

"What plan?" He had some vague idea of what Chloe was getting at and it scared the hell out of him.

"It wants to find a permanent home. It learned enough from Dr. Warren to know that the human body will eventually react to its presence. The high fever, the enlarged heart, the large quantities of adrenaline. Those are all side-effects of its presence and all things that'll kill its human host. That's why it made me steal those drugs. It knew that they would reduce my fever, keep me sedated. The sedating effect would decrease the adrenaline. It would also allow it to take permanent control. The reason I only tried to escape at night was that it could only take control of me at night, while my brain was sleeping. If it could make me sleep all the time, it could have control all the time." She checked his face to see if he was understanding it all.

"How do you know all this?" Trina inquired. She had stepped to the mirror and was staring straight out at them, her hands cupped around her face to block out the light coming from behind her.

"From when it was talking to me. I didn't hear specific words and stuff. I got impressions. The large growth in my head? That's to enable it to gain control over the brain. It allows this thing to produce the sort of responses it needs, whether it be psychic powers or incredible strength. It's like a walkie-talkie."

"So, get rid of the tumor and you get rid of the entity?" Jason looked straight at her, wondering just how much she had been made privy to.

"No. If you remove it, like they did from Bryan Warren, then it just grows back."

"Then, how do we stop it?"

"Hell, I don't know. It knew the time to leave me was coming. It sure wasn't going to jeopardize its chances by telling me all its weaknesses."

Jason sank into the desk chair and hung his head in his hands. "So, we're right back where we started. We still don't have a clue how to get rid of this thing."

"Chloe, did you get any sense that the treatments were hurting it any?"

"No, Trina. It didn't seem to be."

"All right then. Jason? I think we're going to have to start a much more radical treatment. That's the only thing I can think of that might even stand a chance of killing this thing." She was doing a great impression of the brave little solder, though her insides had turned to mush.

He stood up and risked looking directly at her, instantly betraying his fear and pity. "What do you want me to do, Trina?"

"So far as the hospital is concerned, Chloe is still the patient here. Nobody comes down here. Understand?"

"Yes."

"You're going to have to call Professor Arnst. They have a portable unit in their cancer ward here and he can borrow it for the treatments. He can take care of any paperwork that needs to be signed, too."

His face was etched in pain, his lips taut and his eyes pressed nearly shut. "Are you sure about this, Trina?"

"No, but what choice do we have?"

"All right. I'll take care of it."

Chloe watched him walk to the back of the room and pull out his cell phone. Then, she approached the window and turned her guilty eyes toward Trina.

"I wish I could have stopped it. You've been so good to me, so kind. Of all the people I know, you and Mr. Callahan are the ones I least wanted to hurt."

Trina placed one palm against the glass and forced herself to smile at Chloe. "I know that, honey. Would it help you any to know that I'm not really suffering from this?"

She overlaid Trina's hand with her own and made a valiant effort to return her smile. "It helps. A little."

"Now, I want to see you take a nap. Your body has been through a lot. You have to give it a chance to heal. Besides, I want you strong enough to go out and celebrate with Jason and me when this thing is all over."

Chloe smiled wanly and mock-saluted. "Yes, ma'am."

She walked slowly, deliberately to the bunk and laid down upon it. She spared one last glance at the window before shutting her eyes but Trina had already retired to her own bed.

Jason returned to them presently, his face still clouded with gloom and his pace slow, plodding. He glanced at Chloe, apparently sound asleep on Trina's cot. Trina herself was lying upon the bed, her arms locked behind her head, her eyes staring at the ceiling.

"Professor Arnst says he can be here at seven o'clock in the morning," Jason explained into the intercom. "They have patients scheduled for the rest of the day but he can be here then. Okay?"

"Sure. I told Chloe to take a nap. She's got to get her strength back. Try to see that she eats something, too. This whole thing must have taken its toll on her."

"Forget Chloe. She's fine now. It's you I'm worried about." Until that very moment, he had had no idea of the depth of his feelings for Trina.

"I feel fine so far. Ask me tomorrow."

He nodded, trying to be positive and reassuring. Truth be told, he was scared to death. He knew what he would do when the time came. He knew for certain that he would gladly offer himself up to the entity, if need be. He knew that he would take it into himself in an instant, if it meant saving Trina.

Jason's internal alarm clock sounded at two in the morning. He had had a difficult time falling asleep. His mind was consumed with worry for Trina, no matter how he tried to banish it from his thoughts. Visions of her face, tortured by the thing and moments away from death tripped across his mental landscape relentlessly. In his own over-burdened brain, he somehow felt that if he could only fall asleep, he would awaken in the morning and find that this whole thing had been no more than a pizza-induced nightmare.

After several hours of unsuccessful attempts at sleep, he finally abandoned the effort in favor of something more constructive. He yawned deeply and trudged to the window to peek in on Trina. She was lying on her side, one leg curled up and one arm tucked under her pillow. For all outward appearances, she seemed just fine.

His mind relieved somewhat, he turned to go back to bed and read. As he began to lower himself onto his bunk, he glanced over to see how Chloe was doing. The covers on her bed were tossed to one side, the pillow fully fluffed and unused. He thought that she must surely be in the bathroom, so he looked in the direction of the door. It was ajar and, in the dim light of the room, he could see that the small bathroom was empty.

His mind turned cartwheels, trying to figure out just where Chloe might have gone. He couldn't imagine that she would just slip out without saying a word. It just wasn't like her.

He hurried back to the window and held down the intercom button. "Trina? Are you awake?"

"I am now. What's up, Jason?"

"Chloe's gone."

"Gone? What do you mean, gone?" She trotted to the window, trying to peer through the murky glass.

"I mean, she's not here. She's not in the bathroom, either."

"Did she leave a note?"

"No," he said before scanning the room for such a note.

"She wouldn't go off without at least leaving a note. Jason, something's wrong."

"I know the feeling." He thought hard for a minute, his head swimming with the intensity of it. Suddenly, his eyes snapped back to Trina. "Trina, when Chloe passed the thing into you, do you remember feeling anything?"

"No. Just some pressure. But I was pretty spooked, so I don't think I'm all that reliable a witness."

"And do you feel anything now? Anything strange, I mean?"

She considered this for a moment, sadly beginning to realize what Jason was getting at. "I don't feel a bit different. Jason, when Chloe was talking to us, explaining about the entity and how it worked, I seem to remember that she referred to you as 'Mr. Callahan'. She's been calling you by your first name ever since that first day."

"And she cursed. Trina, are you thinking what I'm thinking?"

Trina, her eyes wide and her lips tightly pursed, cocked her head in furious realization. "I'm thinking that it tricked us. It had control of her from the moment she fell asleep last night and used her to fool us into thinking that it had passed into me."

"And now it's on the loose out there, possibly transferring to someone else in order to throw us off its track."

"Let me out, Jason. We've got to find her."

He stepped to the crank and forced it to turn in his hand. "What if it's already made the exchange?"

Trina grabbed up her clothes and headed for the bathroom, closing the door only partially so she could dress. "If it's already transferred, then we should see the tell-tale burn mark."

"But if it made a direct transfer, like it supposedly did with you, then there wouldn't be a burn mark."

"Pray that isn't so, Jason."

She darted out of the bathroom and grabbed her cell phone from where it rested on the desk. Shoving it into her pocket, she jerked open the door to the main hallway

"Be careful, Jason. Remember, this thing can read our thoughts."

He nodded, that chilling fact hitting home as he stepped into the hallway with no idea whatsoever where Chloe might be or what she might already have done. His blood turned to ice as he further realized that this entity would do anything – anything at all – to survive. They were all expendable. Even Chloe.

"My first and best guess is to check the hospital's pharmacy. Maybe it needs to replace the drugs that it tried to take from Gulf Coast."

"That sounds right, Jason. You check there. I'll alert security. Get them to seal off the building."

Jason and Trina separated, he turning left off the elevator

and she right. As he approached the glass window of the pharmacy with its foot-tall lettering, he noticed that the door was ever so slightly ajar. Gun drawn, he eased the door open several more inches, peering into the half-dark and waiting for his eyes to adjust.

"Chloe? Are you in here?"

He took one small step inside the door, still trying to make out anything at all in the dim light. For a second, he thought that he had heard the sound of someone lurking in the back, but then all was silent again. Two more steps, his heart marking each with a dozen beats. Then, the world went from gray to black.

Something hit him from behind, something hard and unyielding. He had heard nothing behind him, had sensed no presence that close to him. And yet Chloe, who had long since heard his thoughts, was crouching in the shadows, waiting to spring.

She allowed the metal-framed chair to drop onto the tiles, then picked up the paper bag full of pills and fled. She shut the wooden door as she left, giving the appearance that all was still well at the pharmacy.

Leisurely, she walked down the hall, her street clothes and serene appearance allowing her to pass for normal. The thing had total control of her now. Whatever part of Chloe that remained ensconced in her body was now deeply hidden and frightfully reduced to the role of observer.

She passed several people on her way to the main entrance. The general idea was to gain the parking lot, take a car and get far enough away from there that it would be afforded enough time to transfer to another host. This woman's body was still far from depleted but it had become more of a hindrance than a help.

The paper bag full of drugs was concealed safely inside her denim jacket. She marched confidently toward the front door, now only several yards from attaining her goal.

"Excuse me, ma'am," said the security guard as he stepped into her path. "I'm afraid we're having a small problem. You won't be able to leave the building just now."

She eyed him peculiarly, appraising his strength and speed with her keen eyes. "Whyever not?" she asked, unswayed.

"A patient has come up missing. Until we find her, we can't allow anyone to leave the building."

She stood, rooted to the spot, for just a moment longer, then she lashed out with one deceptively thin arm. The guard was knocked backward, his arms flailing in an attempt to catch his balance. As he was forced to admit that all hope of that had long since passed, one hand traveled to his holster and snatched out his gun.

"Hold it right there!" he barked, his other hand reaching for his walkie-talkie. "I think we've found her. Main entrance. Hurry."

The poor man managed to right himself, thinking that he had momentarily gained an advantage over her. Chloe stood before him, a supposedly weak, witless opponent. Placing one index finger between her teeth, she giggled girlishly and batted her lashes.

"You can't hurt me. Go ahead and try. I won't move. Honest." Her voice was lilting, hypnotic.

The guard stood his ground, the gun still leveled at her, though he doubted his own ability to use it.

That was all Chloe needed. With one last giggle, she simply turned on her heel and strode toward the door, pausing there just long enough to waggle her fingers at him and wink. When she turned back toward the door, Trina stood on the other side of it, her steely eyes trained on Chloe.

"Stop right there, Chloe. Or whoever you are. There's no way you're leaving this hospital." Trina was unmoving, unblinking. In one hand, she clutched a small bag; in the other, an amulet. She fought hard to keep her mind a blank.

"Don't be absurd, Miss Dane. You of all people should know I can't be hurt. Why don't you step aside before I hurt *you*." The voice issuing from Chloe's mouth was still musical, almost enthralling in its resonance.

"Unlike that guard, I'll kill you if I have to."

"I admire your bravery, Miss Dane. Really I do. But you've seen for yourself that this body can't be hurt. That security guard at Gulf Coast shot me. An hour later, there wasn't much more than a pin-hole in me. Now, step aside before I kill you." Her eyes – like her voice – had gone from serene to murderous.

"Freeze, Chloe!" the voice behind her shouted.

She didn't even bother to turn around to look. "Hello, Mr. Callahan. Come to save your fair lady?"

"Chloe, step away from the door. You're not leaving this hospital, so you might as well come back to the basement."

"Fools! Chloe isn't here anymore. She can't hear you and she can't see you. I can. And what I see are two frightened, ineffectual humans. Stand aside."

She moved to brush past Trina but Trina stubbornly blocked her way. She offered far more resistance than the thing had intuited her capable of. Exerting more force, it was able to back her against the wall and wrap Chloe's fingers around her throat. A shot rang out from behind and slightly to the right, though Chloe's body wasn't even staggered by it.

The pressure continued to increase on Trina's wind pipe. Trina's fisted hands batted at the woman's arms but to no avail. At once, Jason leaped onto Chloe's back, tightening his own grip on her throat. The thing was steadfast, taking only a moment to swing one arm and relieve itself of the fly which had landed on its back. Then, it returned to choking Trina.

In one enormous effort, Jason picked up a nearby metal astray and swung it with all his might at Chloe's head. He distinctly heard the crackle of bone matter somewhere inside Chloe skull, then saw her eyes momentarily glaze over. That small window of opportunity was not lost on Jason. He moved in swiftly, throwing the entire weight of his body against Chloe's dazed form and knocking her against the wall. At last freed, Trina staggered to the nearby vending machine and leaned against it, trying to regain her air.

Jason was lying in a bruised heap on the cement walkway outside the hospital's electric door. Chloe had managed to pull herself along the stucco wall until she finally achieved full standing status. In this position, her head bowed and her arms bracing her against the wall, she swung her head at an impossible angle, her hot eyes targeting Jason's recovering form.

She seized the lapels of his jacket and hauled him from the ground, the other hand grasping onto his gun, lost in the scuffle but now lying nearer Chloe than Jason. Growling preternaturally, she pressed his already aching body against the hard wall savagely, bringing the gun to within inches of his chin.

"You're very stupid, Mr. Callahan. Pity you won't have the time to work on that flaw."

She cocked the gun with one easy jerk and placed a thin finger on the trigger. The vicious face struggled for a while, caught between a sinister sneer and tear-flooded eyes. One second beast, the next second angel, Jason was in doubt as to which would win.

The gun began to tremble as everything around them sank into the landscape, unnoticed by either and pitifully inactive. The gun trembled. The entity's determination wavered as Chloe's control winked in and out.

"No," she whispered, her eyes looking momentarily sad before being overshadowed by murderous cunning. "Can't..."

Her lip quivered and her hand began to shake, the gun nearly slipping through her limp fingers and onto the pavement. Then, as suddenly as Chloe had appeared, she also disappeared, making way for the entity to complete its malevolent mission. The metamorphosis complete, it pulled Jason several inches away from the wall, reasserting its control and punctuating its speech.

"Now! I will finish it!"

Its grip on the gun tightened, the finger pressed ever harder on the trigger. Still, Jason stared it down, daring it to shoot, trying to erase the fear from his frayed mind. Behind him, Trina had regained her composure. She stood, feet firmly planted, lips working at words that grew ever louder. Her hand, fisted around something, was raised, ready. Whatever language she spoke was foreign to Jason; he had no idea what she was up to. But he prayed that it would work.

Chloe's will tried to assert itself again. Her body began to teeter madly and her fingers weakened on the gun. Slowly, her head shook back and forth, her mouth dropping into a small circle and her eyes pleading for help.

"Jason," she muttered in an agonizing moan.

"Chloe! Fight it!" he coached forcefully.

She studied his eyes for a moment, a hint of recognition seeping into her own. "No," she stated simply, one tiny tear rolling down her cheek.

Like a bolt of lightning, her hand jerked the gun around, pressing the muzzle against her own throat. At the same instant, she pulled back on the trigger, her eyes still open and aware.

Behind her, Trina froze, mid incantation, her efforts aborted, all hope lost.

The bullet passed clean through her neck, penetrating the vending machine behind her and bathing Trina in a spray of blood. Her body teetered there, bathed in a shower of sparks. Her eyes adopted a crystal clarity just then, something akin to rapture as a fast-fading smile ran across her pale face. And then she fell.

Trina snapped into action at once, dropping hard onto the cement beside Chloe's limp body. "Everyone out of this area. I don't want anybody within a hundred yards of here."

People scattered in all directions, stunned by the gore-ridden still life before them but still protective of their own health. Security guards helped push back the stragglers, their eyes flitting back to the little scenario every now and again.

"Quick! Let's get her to the basement. If she dies here, that thing will just transfer to a new host."

Trina heeded his warning, grabbing Chloe's heals and hefting her off the pavement. Together, they ran to the elevator, people scurrying out of their path in horror.

Seconds mutated into hours as the elevator traveled toward the basement at an impossibly slow pace. When they reached the basement, they raced toward the isolation room, bearing Chloe along as fast as they could. It wasn't until they had placed her on the bed and shut the door that they felt relatively safe.

Still panting desperately for air, the agents leaned against the door and tried to recover whatever was left of their sanity. They craned their necks precariously to look at each other, both faces possessed of the same inarguable fear.

"Now what?" Jason wanted to know. "Do we just let her lay there and die?"

"Well, by all rights, we should. I mean, this is the second time she's tried to kill herself."

"Trina, it's a simple through-and-through. If we patch her up and give her some more blood, we might save her."

"Save her? From what? Peace? Heaven?"

He searched her eyes for understanding; found none. "All right then. It's agreed?"

"Agreed."

They walked tentatively to the window and chanced a look at the motionless Chloe. She did look peaceful, released from her torment and hopefully from her tormentor. There was no tell-tale burn mark; no sign that Chloe had died or that the entity had left her body. They stood there, lost between pity and guilt, and watched for signs of both deaths.

Chapter Ten

Jason and Trina had watched Chloe's motionless body for several hours, first with their noses pressed against the mirror, then over coffee on Jason's bunk. By the time they had finally decided that Chloe was well and goodly dead, it was too late to be of any use. Besides, there was still no sign that the entity had left Chloe's body; no signs that it had also ceased to exist. Trina had been weeping off and on since the door had first shut.

And so, with sadness at Chloe's death snapping at their heels, they had turned in for the night, determined to dispose of the body properly if, upon awakening, there was still no sign of life or of the entity.

Several hours later, a loud crash at the mirror terrified them from their sleep. Bolt upright in their bunks, they leveled their eyes at the glass. To their mystification, there stood Chloe, pressing her face to the glass and trying to make her brown eyes see whatever might be on the other side.

"Can you guys hear me out there?" She waited for a moment for them, far too stunned to speak, to respond to her calls. "Hey! Are you guys still out there?"

"Chloe! We're here." Jason dashed to the window and switched on the lights. "My God! I can't believe you're still alive."

"Neither can I," she laughed. It was a warm and welcome sound in the silence of the dark. "I thought this time I was a goner for sure."

"How do you feel?" Trina asked, peering in at her with something akin to reverence.

"I feel fine. That thing's still in here with me, though. I hurt it bad when I shot myself but it seems to be recovering."

"We figured you for dead. How in God's name did you ever survive?"

"God had nothing to do with this, Jason. It was all that creature's doing." She yawned placidly and rubbed her arms. "I'm sorry for all of this. When I think how close I came to shooting you..." She broke off in a savage shiver.

"You didn't almost shoot me, Chloe. It did."

A giant chasm of silence opened between them, each standing in a puddle of their own thoughts. Chloe checked their eyes, watching them look at each other for support.

"You two didn't try to revive me this time. How's come?" She asked purely out of curiosity. No malice was intended.

"We just figured that, after everything you'd been through, it was what you wanted."

She cocked her mouth off to one side thoughtfully and nodded. "Yep. You were right about that."

"Do you need anything, Chloe?" Trina inquired, her eyes soft with sadness and guilt.

"Well, I am kinda hungry. Shooting yourself tends to take a lot out of a girl."

"Can't you make it yourself?" Jason wondered out loud.

"I 'spose. I just thought it weirded you out to have me do that. Besides, my house guest is feeling kinda under the weather right at the moment."

He nodded contemplatively. "What's your pleasure?"

"Anything, as long as it's hot."

Jason pulled on his jacket and disappeared through the door, bound for the cafeteria. Trina stayed close to the mirror, eyeing Chloe every now and again. In much the same way, Chloe was watching her. The two women suddenly felt ill at ease with each other, strangely alien. Finally, Chloe walked straight up to the mirror and glared out at Trina.

"Who peed in your Wheaties?" she asked jokingly.

"What?"

"What's got your underwear in a bunch? What's bugging you?"

"The whole affair. I have to admit, after everything that

happened earlier, I'm a little afraid of you."

"I can understand that. But it's just little ol' me, Chloe. For the moment at least."

"Can you still hear my thoughts?"

"Faintly. But my psychic powers are a little out of whack. I just tried to turn on the TV, but no dice."

"And can you hear the voices? The others?"

"Both at the moment."

"What was it like...when that thing took control over you?"

She paced a bit, a slow and methodical plodding that bought her time to think. "It was kinda like watching a movie. I could see everything that was going on and hear everything and all. I just couldn't do anything about it."

"So, you knew that it was trying to trick us into believing that it had taken possession of me?"

"Yeah." She cast her eyes down to the floor in contrition. "But I tried to send you messages. I kept cussing over and over to myself. See, this thing sorta needs me, too. It needs to learn things from me in order to exist in the world. It has to know my mind in order to convince you that it's really me. It's kind of a...a...symbiotic relationship." She smiled, happy to have remembered that one obscure word.

"And that's why it used the curse words while it was talking to us. It heard you saying them and thought that was the way you spoke."

"Yeah. That's why. But no matter how I tried to get up out of that pit it had me in, I couldn't do anything to stop it. Until I saw that it was going to kill Jason. I couldn't let it do that. Not ever. But I had to blank out my thoughts, my presence, in order to be able to pull it off. And the only way I could think of to stop it from killing Jason was to make it kill us. I know it could have gone into somebody else after I was dead. But there wasn't any other way out. I think I would have put almost anybody in danger to save Jason."

"And for that I will be eternally grateful," Jason crowed as he stepped into the room. "I hope you like egg salad. The pickings down at Ye Olde Cafeteria are pretty slim at this hour of the morning."

"Egg salad's fine."

"Good. I also got you some pudding and some soup and some cake and...oh, yes...a couple of candy bars."

She giggled coyly into her hand. "I can't believe you brought all this back for me."

"Hey, only the best for the girl who saved my life. Trina, I brought us some coffee and soup, too. Figured we could use a little fuel in our tanks."

She took one of the coffee cups from him and removed the lid. "I don't think any of us are going to get much sleep from here on out. We've still got to figure out how to get that thing out of Chloe. And I think we need a few new rules around here."

"Such as?"

"Such as, neither of us goes in there unless the other is out here. And under no circumstances is Chloe to ever leave that room."

"Sounds right." He held up the bag of food, waving it in front of the mirror for effect. "Just let me get my suit on and I'll bring this to you."

She smiled and nodded eagerly, then stood well back from the door while he opened it. He barely took one step inside, placing the bag on the floor and then backing out of the room. Once he had closed the door and walked to the mirror, he had a sad, sheepish look on his face.

"Don't worry, Jason. I understand that you're scared of me. Heck, I'm scared of me. Face it. I'm a freak."

"Well, let's just try to figure out how to rob you of your freakdom. Let's go over everything we know, right from the beginning."

She unwrapped the sandwich and took the lid off the soup. In one enormous bite, she easily devoured a quarter of the sandwich, pausing to chew only moments before speaking.

"Okay. Where did this thing come from?" she mumbled, her speech impaired by the amount of food still in her mouth.

"I'm not exactly sure where it originated. But we do know that Professor Stillman discovered it at an archaeological dig in Malaysia."

"Discovered it? Where exactly, Jason?" She drank from the cup of soup, wiping her mouth on the back of her hand.

"In a tomb. A man had been buried there centuries ago. Evidently, the thing had taken possession of him and the other villagers sealed him up in that tomb so that he couldn't harm anyone else. The pictographs that Professor Stillman discovered there told the tale, but not how to get rid of it."

"Hm. That's when it entered his son's body?"

"Apparently."

"It obviously couldn't escape from the crypt," Trina added quietly. "Otherwise, it would have gone in search of a new host."

"Why? Why couldn't it get out of the crypt?" Jason stared thoughtfully into the distance, his coffee cup paused in midair.

"Because it was air-tight?" Trina offered plaintively.

"Yes. Exactly. And it would have been in there for several hundred years without a human host and...supposedly...without air."

Chloe was watching their exchange from behind the glass, listening intently while she finished her food.

"Which means, Trina, that it doesn't require oxygen. It can survive without oxygen but not without a host."

"If it needed a host to survive, then how come it was still alive when they opened that tomb all those centuries later?"

Trina and Jason's eyes turned to Chloe, startled by her sudden entrance into the conversation.

"That's a good question, Jason. Why?"

"Trina, if you bury someone alive, which would kill him first? Starvation, lack of water, or lack of oxygen?" Jason's eyes were gleaming with wild anticipation.

"He'd suffocate first. Why?"

"He'd use up all the oxygen and then die."

"That's generally what suffocation means."

"Which would mean that the tomb was nearly devoid of oxygen. That's why the thing was able to survive. It doesn't need a human host to support life. It needs a human host to protect it from the oxygen in our atmosphere. That's why it had to transfer from one body to the next so fast. And why it leaves that trail of burnt ground. It bursts into flames when it comes into contact with oxygen."

"Or light," Trina suggested. "What if light hurts it? Like a vampire or something."

"No," Jason insisted. "Chloe, was it dark when you and Brenda had your little scuffle?"

"No. It was still light out. Daylight saving time, you know."

"It's oxygen. Expose it to oxygen and it dies."

"That's all well and good, Jason, but how do we get it out of Chloe's body in order to expose it to the air?"

"Do I have to think of everything?" he asked comically, gesturing wildly with his hands.

"Something made that thing leave Bryan Stillman's body in favor of his mother's. And Bryan is the only person alive who knows what."

"I'm way ahead of you, Trina." Jason grabbed his phone off the desk and hurriedly dialed the Stillman's number. "I'd like to speak to Bryan," he informed the voice that answered.

"Can I ask who's calling?"

"It's Jason Callahan."

"Callahan?! Why in God's name are you calling at this hour? Do you know what time it is here?" Professor Stillman seemed quite incensed at this intrusion.

"I'm sorry, Professor. My partner and I are very close to finding a way to kill this entity. But we need Bryan's help."

There was a long silence at the other end of the line. Then Professor Stillman sighed heavily. "Very well. Just one minute."

Jason waited impatiently for Bryan to reach the phone. He shook his foot nervously, crossing and re-crossing his legs.

"Yes?"

"Bryan?"

"This is he. Can I help you, Mr. Callahan?"

"I was wondering, on the day that the entity left your body, what were you doing?"

"It's like my father already told you. I was just watching TV with my mom."

Jason's shoulders slumped a bit, but he kept pressing. "Talk me through it, one step at a time from the moment you entered the room."

"Let's see now. I came out of the kitchen with a Coke. I sat next to my mother on the sofa. She already had the TV on, so I never touched the remote. We talked for a couple of minutes, then she picked up the channel guide. She said that it was too dark to read, so I reached over to turn on the lamp next to me. When I did, sparks flew out of the switch and this stinging sensation shot up my arm."

"There was a short in the light switch?" Jason asked eagerly, his eyes shooting to Trina.

"I guess. I'm no electrician, but I suppose that's right."

"And right after that, that's when the thing left you?"

"Yes. My body started to jerk and I kind of jumped back on the couch. You know, trying to get away from the lamp in case it exploded or something. Then I got this real weird feeling, like I was falling down a deep hole. Tunnel vision, I guess they call it. The next thing I knew, I could see myself grabbing my mother and kissing her, although I didn't have any control over it. Then, she was just lying there on the couch, unconscious. The thing was in her and I was free."

"Thank you, Bryan. You've been more help than you could ever know."

Bryan yawned groggily. "I hope your friend will be okay. I'd sure like to see you fry this thing, whatever it is."

"Thanks to you, I think we can do that now. Good-bye, Bryan."

Jason switched off the phone and placed it gently on the desk. He stared first at Trina, then at Chloe, his smile only hinting at what he now knew.

"What?!" the two women shouted in chorus.

"Electricity."

"Electricity?" Trina marveled.

"Just before the entity left Bryan's body, he reached over to turn on a lamp. He got a shock from the short in the wiring, and the thing just abandoned him."

"Then, you've got to electrocute me?" Chloe asked in despair. It sounded like a not-at-all pleasant thing to have to go through.

"Nothing that drastic. Maybe just a little jolt."

"Like shock therapy. Only your brain won't be fried when we're done."

"Thanks, Trina. It's good to know who your friends are."

"We can suit her up, then administer a light shock. When the entity leaves her body, she can put on the suit and just wait until it dies from exposure."

"That's assuming the suit really will keep the thing out."

"Well, it's the best shot we've got. Why not go ahead with it?"

"Uh...excuse me?" Chloe prompted in a tremulous voice. "Are you two sure you know what you're doing? I mean, I don't want to end up a rutabaga or anything."

"Don't worry, Chloe. We wouldn't do anything that would hurt you. Would we, Trina?"

"No. Of course not." She had meant that in all sincerity, though her preoccupied mind just couldn't put the proper inflection to it. You see, in her own mind, she wasn't exactly sure she could do it. She hadn't a clue just how many volts it would take to drive the thing away. She was flying blind.

Chloe was lying on her bed, having been admonished to rest as much as possible before the big event. All through the day, she had sensed the goings on in the other room. At one point, some ominous-looking equipment had been brought in and, judging from the size of the thing, it could do significant damage to anybody connected to its many wires. Professor Arnst made another appearance, his face grim and his eyes playing keep-away with hers as he worked on the ventilation system. He had connected two tanks of oxygen, enough to make the air in the chamber oxygen-rich, thus speeding the thing's death when it left Chloe.

"So, how's this going to work?" Chloe questioned from her side of the glass partition. "Do I have to lick a light socket or something?"

Trina paused in her computations long enough to cast an

amused grin over her shoulder. "Nothing that dramatic, I assure you. Have you ever seen a movie where someone's heart stopped beating and they used one of those machines with the little paddles to jump-start the heart?"

"Yeah. Where they yell 'clear!' and everybody steps back. Then the guy's body jumps up into the air."

"Well, that's basically what we're going to do to you. Of course, we'll use the lowest possible voltage to begin with."

"Oh, of course," she stated mockingly, her lips pressed tightly together in a little grimace. "We wouldn't want to waste any precious electricity on little old me."

Jason snorted laughter at her and shook his head. "Always with the jokes, eh, Chloe?"

"You know what they say. Laughter is the best medicine." She grew strangely quiet for a moment, she and Jason taking the time to study each other's faces in solemn reverie. When she spoke again, her voice was soft and tremulous. "Just promise me one thing."

"Anything," he muttered.

"This is the last time. If this thing doesn't work, I'm outta here. You do whatever you have to do. Shoot me. Burn me. I don't care. Just don't make me go through this anymore."

Jason twisted up his face, feeling inexplicably near tears in the face of this brave and determined girl. "I promise you this, Chloe: This time, it will work. That thing will leave your body for good. And then you can get on with a normal life."

She nodded slowly, giving due thought to the definition of 'normal'. It seemed to her just now as if normal were some esoteric concept, always meant for other people and always completely unattainable for her. After a few moments had passed, she felt the lump in her throat ease up enough that she could again speak.

"There's a couple of things I want you two to know before we start this."

Jason and Trina gathered at the mirror like visitors to an aquarium. They listened quietly and intently, completely unsure of what Chloe would say next.

"The two of you have been so good to me. So kind and so

brave." She broke off in tears, fighting them, losing. "My family was never as good to me as you two have been. I don't want that to pass unnoticed. I've never been the brightest person, or the prettiest or the richest. Heck, in the course of every-day life, I pass pretty much unnoticed. But you guys have treated me like I was the most important person in the whole world. Like I mattered. You've risked your own lives for me and...well...I just wanted you to know that I appreciate it. More than you'll ever know."

Trina fought her own barrage of tears. Over the past few weeks, she had come to feel so close to Chloe, had been so impressed by her spirit and courage, that she almost felt sorry that it had all come to an end. Her life would feel somehow a little less full without Chloe in it on a daily basis.

"Chloe," she began, her smile faltering as the corners of her mouth trembled, "I think you have more courage, more spirit and love in you than any ten people I've ever met. If this had happened to anyone but you, it would have killed them."

"Well, if I've been brave, it's only because of the two of you. Now, enough of the hearts and flowers. On with the show." She had spent far too much time wallowing in her self-pity; had bared far too much of her heart. Truth be told, she felt more love for the two people on the other side of that glass than she ever had for any other person in her life.

"We're ready when you are. Just give us a chance to suit up."

She abandoned the mirror in deference to the bed. For some reason, now that the moment was upon her, she was beginning to lose faith. That, and the use of her legs. She strode silently to the bed and lay upon it, staring blindly up at the ceiling and counting the little dimples in the tile.

"Okay, hon," Jason soothed, rubbing her arm and grinning down at her. "We're both here with you. And don't worry. When it comes to shocking a person, Trina is the best."

Trina shot him a mean look and then switched on the machine. "Now, I know you have a history of re-animating yourself, so I hope you can manage that just one more time. If we have to use high-voltage, it might just send you into cardiac arrest."

"Don't sweat the small stuff, Trina. If I don't come back as me, I'll come back as a horse. You can bring me sugar and ride me on the weekends." Her face was full of good humor and light. It made Trina giggle just to see it.

"We're ready, then?"

"Ready as ready can be. Hit me with the juice, Bruce."

She laid her arms at her sides, subconsciously gripping the edge of the bed with one hand. She wasn't exactly sure what this would feel like, but she was sure it would not feel entirely pleasant.

Trina charged the machine and checked Jason's face. More than anything, it was he who leant her strength right then. "Hold on to your hats. Jason, you keep well back from her."

Jason rooted himself to the floor several feet away from the bed but still near enough that he could see the beads of sweat trickling down Chloe's forehead. Trina watched her equipment carefully, waiting until the defibrillator was completely charged. Then, she did the deed.

The instant that the paddles made contact with Chloe's chest, Chloe felt a sick feeling begin in the pit of her stomach. Her chest tickled where the paddles had touched and her body felt as though it had somehow been frozen in time for several seconds. Outside of that, she felt no other ill effects.

"Chloe? Are you all right?" Trina frowned at the girl, disappointed that there had been no outward signs of the entity's departure.

"I'm fine. Kind of giddy, though. I feel like..." Her face locked into a rictus of pain, small tears squeezing out from behind her lids. She grabbed her head with both hands and tried valiantly to ball herself up.

"Chloe? What's wrong?" Trina touched her arm, trying to get her to relax her muscles and open her eyes.

"Head," she moaned. "Hurts." She could form no more words for quite some time. She could only fight the horrible vice-like pain in her head and whine. "Do it again." She managed this from behind clenched teeth, her eyes still not daring to open.

"Are you sure?"

"Do it!" she bellowed, at once collapsing from the pain.

Trina raised the voltage several notches and recharged the defibrillator. She checked Jason's face, then stared momentarily at Chloe's closed eyes. Before she could talk herself out of it, she clamped the paddles down on Chloe's chest, causing it to jump into the air in a little dance of flight.

Chloe screamed mightily, an agonizing, murderous sound. Then, her wide and haunting eyes turned on Trina. She looked for a second as though she might say something, then her mouth simply flew open as though some force other than Chloe's own musculature was at work.

As her mouth opened, looking for all the world as if she were trying to vomit, an unbelievably powerful rush of air flew at Jason and Trina, staggering them backward and frightening them badly. They exchanged horrified glances, then turned their eyes on Chloe. She was lying very still on the bed, too afraid to move.

"Was that it?" Trina asked Jason in a weak voice.

"It must have been," he intoned, pointing one trembling finger at the bed sheets.

As Trina allowed her eyes to travel to the bed, she spied the edge of the pillow case immediately next to Chloe's face. It was not just burnt but rather simply gone. There was a fresh white pillowcase covering the pillow, then it simply ended, exposing a wretched charred pillow beneath.

"Dear God!" Trina gasped, marveling at the sight. "It's a wonder she wasn't hurt."

"Huh?" Chloe finally asked, her brow knitted and her eyes searching for the source of their consternation. Finally, she spotted the missing expanse of pillowcase and she swooned as if she might pass out. "Lord!"

"So, where is it now? Still here?"

"Did anybody feel anything strange?" Jason asked, glancing about the room as if he expected to see the thing hovering over their heads, waiting to pounce.

"No. I feel fine." Trina inspected her suit, checking for signs of forced entry. "Not a mark on me. How about..." Her mouth dropped open in mid-sentence as she realized that the singe mark trailed off the pillowcase, down the side of the bed and all the way across the floor.

Jason had noticed it, too, for he was even now tracing the mark across the room. The asbestos floor tiles had not simply burnt. They were disintegrated. The mark ended abruptly at the door and so Jason pressed his face harshly against the small glass window in an attempt to inspect the floor outside.

"Oh, dear God! It didn't..." Trina had come up behind him and was staring at the back of his head.

"No. The floor outside looks untouched. Whatever happened to it must have happened right here."

They both stared in wonderment at the bottom of the door where a slight indentation was punctuated by a large spattering of soot and ash. A shiver went up their spines. The ancient linoleum tiles beneath it were gone, burned away to reveal the concrete slab beneath.

"So, I'm okay?" Chloe had by now recovered from her headache and was propped up on both elbows staring at them questioningly.

"I'm not sure," Trina said, eyeing the girl warily as she approached the bed. "How do you feel?"

"Lonely. I haven't been alone in this body for a couple of weeks now. It feels kind of lonely."

Trina wrapped a cuff around her arm and inflated it. She shrugged her shoulders at the results and then removed the cuff. "Your pressure's fine. And your heart rate seems to have slowed. Did you feel anything when it left you?"

"It screamed in my head. The first time you shocked me, it screamed like it had been hurt something fierce. That's why I told you to do it again. And when you did it the second time, I suddenly felt like I was going to explode. That's how bad it wanted out of me."

"The only question is, is it dead?" Jason crossed his arms over his chest and glanced about the room.

"The results of your CAT scan are back," Dr. Walker said as he strode into Chloe's hospital room. "The growth seems to be almost completely gone."

Chloe beamed at him, her eyes twinkling with relief and joy. "Then, I can go home?"

"I don't see why not. As far as I can tell, you're healthy as a horse."

For a moment, Chloe's smile faded and she looked pitifully disappointed. "You haven't seen Jason or Trina anywhere, have you?"

"Did I hear someone mention my name?"

Her face lit up as she spied Jason in the doorway. "Jason! There you are! I thought maybe I'd lost my charm once I became dispossessed."

He laughed whole-heartedly and shook his head. "Not a chance. I brought you a present. Trina?"

Chloe craned her neck to watch Trina enter the room, wondering what all the secrecy was about. As Trina rounded the doorway, she held out both her hands. In them rested a small gray kitten, its eyes huge and deeply green.

"We didn't want you to be lonely without us. So, we brought you a little friend."

"You'll be happy to know that this kitten was rescued from the animal shelter. Oh, and it's a boy." He watched her take the small animal and cuddle it to her chest.

"Well, then, I can think of only one thing to name it. Jason." She smiled smartly up at him, stroking the kitten's fur and scratching its ears.

"That's a terrible thing to do to a sweet little kitten. Whatever happened to names like Fluffy or Muffin?"

"The same thing that happened to names like Olive and Gertrude."

A slight hush passed over the room as they basked in the warmth and relief of a world which had once again become normal. Then, Chloe began to tear up, anticipating her friends' impending exit.

"So, where are you two off to next? Some wildly exciting case, I imagine. A haunted house, perhaps? Or maybe vampires?"

"Haven't a clue," Trina sighed. "One thing about this job: You never know what to expect."

"Well, I hope you'll look me up if you're ever in the area

again. Drop in and I'll cook you breakfast. Of course, you might just have to share your sausage with Little Jason here."

"We'll be sure to keep in touch. You two take care of each other, now." Trina leaned in and kissed Chloe on the forehead.

"And just remember one thing, young lady." Jason waited for Chloe to offer her undivided attention. "Don't take any rides from strangers. Oh, and you'd better take very good care of that kitten. You don't want to disappoint us. You could be repossessed."

Everyone in the room groaned at Jason's lame joke. Everyone except Chloe, that is. She laughed heartily, her blue eyes twinkling madly.

About the Author

Patricia Lee Macomber is the former editor-in-chief of ChiZine. She has been published in "Cemetery Dance" magazine and such anthologies as "Shadows Over Baker Street," "Little Red Riding Hood In the Big Bad City," and "Dark Arts." Currently, she lives in North Carolina with her husband, David, and their children.

CROSSROAD
PRESS

www.ingramcontent.com/pod-product-compliance
Lightning Source LLC
Chambersburg PA
CBHW061241170626
46809CB00007B/2777

* 9 7 8 1 9 4 9 9 1 4 9 1 7 *